Advance Praise for

MURDER
Returns to the
PRECIPICE

An endlessly delightful tale and band of characters . . .

—Kirkus Reviews

Murder Returns to the Precipice is brimming with promise and peril—a richly textured mystery that's both charmingly atmospheric and cunningly staged. Be forewarned: Like the coastal waters of Maine, this story will lull you in with its seeming tranquility only to sweep you away in the undercurrent. Take a deep breath and surrender yourself fully. Penny Goetjen is a mighty force!

—John Valeri, Criminal Element

Other Titles by Penny Goetjen

The Empty Chair ~ Murder in the Caribbean

Murder on the Precipice

Murder beyond the Precipice

MURDER
Returns to the
PRECIPICE

PENNY GOETJEN

SECRET
HARBOR
PRESS

For information about this title or to order other books and/or electronic media, contact the publisher:
Secret Harbor Press, LLC
www.secretharborpress.com

Library of Congress Control Number: 2019905159

Printed in the United States of America

Publisher's Cataloging-In-Publication Data
(Prepared by The Donohue Group, Inc.)

Names: Goetjen, Penny, author.

Title: Murder returns to the precipice / Penny Goetjen.

Description: [Charleston, South Carolina] : Secret Harbor Press, [2019]

Identifiers: ISBN 9781733143905 (softcover) | ISBN 9781733143912 (ebook)

Subjects: LCSH: Hotelkeepers--Maine--Boothbay Harbor--Fiction. | Intelligence officers--Maine--Boothbay Harbor--Fiction. | Murder--Investigation--Maine--Boothbay Harbor--Fiction. | Bed and breakfast accommodations--Maine--Boothbay Harbor--Fiction. | Families--Maine--Boothbay Harbor--Fiction. | LCGFT: Detective and mystery fiction. | Thrillers (Fiction)

Classification: LCC PS3607.O3355 M873 2019 (print) | LCC PS3607.O3355 (ebook) | DDC 813/.6--dc23

To my grandmother, who taught me to make delectable chocolate fudge in the kitchen of her creaky old house in Maine and was the inspiration for sweet Amelia Pennington.

CHAPTER ONE

At first glance, it looked like she was resting between reps. Wavy blonde hair hung lifeless several inches below the bench. Her limp arms bent at the elbow, and the tips of her fingers touched the floor. Low music played on the speakers meant for general consumption in an otherwise quiet fitness center.

Elizabeth stepped into the doorway and crept toward her, not intending to interrupt her workout, halting a few feet away. Then she noticed what was very wrong with the picture: the oversized barbell wedged into her neck, carving a grotesque indentation.

Lunging toward the bar, Elizabeth grabbed the stack of circular weights on one end and heaved it up, flipping it off of her. The discs rattled as they bounced on the floor with a thud.

Frantic to find signs of life, Elizabeth splayed one hand on her chest and pressed fingertips on the other under the woman's jawbone. "Oh, God. No." Snatching her cell, she punched in 9-1-1 and switched it to speaker before dropping it to the floor. By the time the dispatcher came on and asked the nature of her emergency, she'd performed a dozen or more chest compressions and inserted two puffs of air. In a focused fog, she kept the resuscitation attempt going until EMTs arrived and forcibly removed her from the victim's side. Stumbling to a vantage point nearby, she looked on helplessly while they continued where she'd left off. Without missing a beat, they moved the young woman to a stretcher and wheeled her away.

Suddenly the music seemed to blare from the corners of the ceiling, so Elizabeth opened the closet that held the electronics and silenced it. She slid onto the seat of a rowing machine near the door. There was no stale sour smell to speak of that was often pervasive in older gyms, just the pungent odor from the new rubber floor. As she waited in the stillness of the room, shook to the core by the grisly image in her head, she slid ever so slightly back and forth on the seat of the erg like a mother trying to soothe a fussy baby.

Before long, the deputy showed up and poked his head through the door, looking to get her story in the awkwardness between former classmates who hadn't connected in years. Sam Austin was the son of the former chief who'd seen firsthand the heartache the Pennington family had endured over decades within the old walls of the inn.

The deputy's shoulders drooped as he removed his high-crowned, pinched hat and crossed the threshold, his eyes trained on the weights as he neared the bench, undoubtedly having been briefed on his way over. Except for the errant barbell, nothing looked out of place. Elizabeth was eager to get the abhorrent task over with.

"Deputy—"

"Please, Elizabeth. We've known each other too long. It's Sam. Just like in school."

With his close-cropped beard, he resembled a ship captain—just needed a skipper's hat with a gold embroidered anchor and a pipe sticking out of the corner of his mouth with smoke encircling his head. But she wasn't aware of anyone in his family who'd earned his living on the ocean. The Austins had a long history in law enforcement.

"Of course, Sam—and it's Lizzi. I was just trying to—"

"I know. You were just trying to help me feel like I belong behind this badge." He tapped the shiny gold shield on his dark brown standard-issue shirt.

"Well, of course you do. You've earned your way here. Walked in your father's footsteps. I was addressing you as you deserved to be."

"Elizabeth . . . you're an amazing woman. Always kind to me. And I appreciate that. More than you'll ever know."

Uncomfortable with where he was heading, she redirected the conversation. "And your father was an incredible man. I'm eternally grateful to him. He saved my life last summer. . . . Happened to stop by to check on the place." She wasn't going to confess it was the first time in almost a year she'd returned since the inn had been ravaged by a Category 4 hurricane. "I'd fallen into the tunnel with no way to get out after the stairway crumbled. No one was around. The place was deserted. I was terrified. Thank God your father showed up and got me out."

"I'm glad you came back. I can't imagine this place if you hadn't returned to bring it back to life. It's so beautiful. It was painful that first year to see it in the condition the storm left it in."

Wondering how often Sam had stopped in to check on the place, she was surprised to hear him express such fondness for the inn. As a youngster, he had tagged along when his father came around. She wondered if it was the inn or the innkeeper's grand-daughter that kept him coming back.

Nodding toward the conspicuously empty bench, she brought them back to her gruesome discovery. "I met her when they checked in yesterday. Cute couple. She asked about the gym . . . if there were free weights, which I thought was odd for a woman, but then I figured—why not? Good for her."

She rose from the erg and sized up the barbell lying perpen-dicular to the bench. Looked like a lot of weight for someone with her frame. Had she been unrealistic in what she could lift? Why hadn't she known to have a spotter when bench pressing?

"They were here to celebrate an anniversary. I don't remember which one." Of course, her grandmother would have recalled. She had a knack for paying attention to details and making connections with her guests. Lizzi had to work on that. "How awful. What a shame for this to happen. I pray she'll be okay." Elizabeth knew the situation appeared dismal, but as the inn's ambassador she had to portray a positive outlook.

"So, she was alone in the gym?" Sam asked.

"She was alone when I walked in. Hard to know how long she'd been here or if anyone else came or went during her workout."

"There are no security cameras?" The deputy glanced to the corners of the ceiling.

"No. We really didn't think it was necessary in here." She used the term "we" loosely. It seemed to carry more weight than saying she'd made the decision on her own. So often during the renovations, she had to cut items off the "would be nice to have" list in order to pay for unexpected overruns. It came down to spending money on only what was necessary. "Besides, I don't think our guests would feel comfortable working out if they knew they were being recorded."

"Well, it certainly would have helped to piece together the sequence of events . . . and the timing."

"Sorry." It was all she could come up with. She regretted the absence of cameras made his job more difficult, but she wasn't going to put them in after the fact, either. "Do you suspect it might not be as straightforward as a simple accident?"

"I have to consider all the possibilities."

"Of course you do."

"Who is she here with?"

Elizabeth gave the officer the name of the woman's husband and their room number, relieved to have him handle breaking the news, but had second thoughts about leaving the grim task to local law enforcement. After all, it was her responsibility as the innkeeper, no matter how uncomfortable it felt. His shoulders seemed to straighten with her offer to accompany him.

At the top of the stairs, she stepped forward to knock on the door. No one answered right away. Could he still be asleep? There probably wasn't a worse way to wake a man than with what this guy was about to hear. She pounded harder, producing a yelp from within. Before long, the unsuspecting husband appeared in a white terry cloth bathrobe, courtesy of the inn—Elizabeth's idea to add a more spa-like feel. The cord of an earbud dangled from one ear; a hand wrapped around an electric toothbrush probed his mustached orifice. His eyes grew wide.

"Sorry to disturb you, Mr. Chase—" Elizabeth began.

He held up an index finger. "Hang on." Leaving the door ajar, he wiped his chin with a sleeve, ducking into the bathroom to drop the appliance inside the door, taking a moment at the sink before reappearing. "Sorry, thought you were my wife. Figured she'd forgotten the room key." He chuckled, pulling the lapels of his robe closer together.

Elizabeth hesitated, suddenly forgetting the words she'd practiced in her head on the way up. All she could manage was, "Mr. Chase, this is Deputy Austin of the Cumberland County Sheriff's Department."

The young man's brows narrowed. "What's this all about?"

Relieved to hear Sam start to speak, she retreated a step, both geographically and mentally.

"Sir, I'm afraid it's about your wife."

"My wife? She's at the gym. Left awhile ago. I would imagine she'd be back soon."

"Yes, sir. I'm afraid there's been an accident . . . in the gym."

"Wh—what do you mean?" He cocked his head like an old man struggling to hear in a crowded room. "What happened? Is she okay?"

"It appears she may have dropped a barbell at some point during her workout."

"Dropped it? Dropped it where?"

"Uh . . . on her neck."

The robed man considered the deputy's words. "Is she okay?" He wasn't grasping the severity of the situation.

"I'm afraid not, sir. She's on the way to the hospital right now."

Elizabeth imagined this might be Sam's first time having to deliver such devastating news in his official capacity.

The husband leaned closer, latching on to the door frame with an oversized hand. "So she's *going* to be okay."

The deputy hesitated. "I would have to defer that determination to the medical professionals."

"Oh God, no." He burst into sobs that seemed to originate from the depths of his gut, making a sickening, mournful sound. She'd never heard anything quite like it—certainly not from a man.

After Sam offered to drive him to the hospital, Elizabeth extended her sincere best wishes and took her leave. Her heart ached for the couple. It was one of those moments where life reminded you so much was out of your control. And life was not going to be fair, so don't expect it.

With such a tragic start, she prayed, with a measure of guilt, it wouldn't cast a shadow on her reign at the inn.

CHAPTER TWO

His presence was felt before the first footfall on the old wooden planks in the foyer. The caravan of cars pulled up to the front, crunching on gravel and kicking up dust, filling the circular drive. He brought a stir to the inn that hadn't been felt for a while—this time it was a positive, exciting stir. The arrival of someone who was rather famous. Elizabeth surveyed the spectacle through the drawing room windows, relieved there were no tour buses in sight. Apparently he was traveling light this trip.

Black Suburbans resembling unmarked government vehicles led the procession, followed by an understated gray limousine—not the stretch kind—a measure of restraint amid the excess. Maybe she would like the guy after all, but she would hold out judgment until she'd a chance to get to know him; that was, if he would allow it.

Like a well-rehearsed, choreographed routine, shiny black doors popped open in unison. But that was where the symmetry ended. Each vehicle emptied out, no two guys dressed alike, a total of seven in all. A couple wore light denim jeans, others donned dark trousers. Most wore sport coats. Hairstyles ranged from non-existent, shiny and bald, to varying lengths of coifs. But none as long as she expected his to be.

One man with a black leather jacket got out of the car closest to the limo and strode back, waving off the driver who had rounded the rear. Instead, the leather jacket grabbed the handle and yanked.

For a fleeting moment, she questioned her sanity for agreeing to what could easily turn out to be a publicity circus, disturbing the serenity of the other guests. Was that a price she was willing to pay? She bent down to stroke her pup, a black Lab mix she'd rescued.

"Hopefully I didn't make a mistake here, Buddy." She could feel his warmth as he leaned against her leg and looked up with wistful brown eyes. "Hard to turn down a reservation for such a large group . . . and for the length of time one goes 'on holiday' from Australia."

Counting on their new marketing strategy of targeting a younger, more active clientele, she hoped they'd be intrigued by a celebrity in their midst and forgiving of any inconvenience generated by his security detail. When it came down to it, just having reopened the doors of the inn after a couple-year hiatus, Elizabeth was grateful for every reservation that came in. She held her breath and prayed the family property, now in her hands, would be as successful as it had been under her parents' and her grandmother's tender care and skillful management.

During post-hurricane renovations, attention had been focused to appeal to the more demanding traveler. The main building sitting high atop the precipice overlooking the open sea to the south was restored to its former New England colonial charm with its white clapboard siding, black shutters, and wraparound front porch. Of the two outbuildings with additional guest rooms, Acadia was spared structural damage owing to the fact it was situated directly behind the main building, which served as a buffer from the wind. With the exception of the exposed western end, repairs had been fairly straightforward and, for the most part, contained to the outside of the building. Moosehead, on the other hand, sitting out in the open, was much more vulnerable and suffered catastrophic damage. After engineers determined it was not salvageable, it was razed, and a larger structure was erected on the footprint to house not only suites, but the fitness center and luxurious spa. With a twinge of guilt, Elizabeth hoped the sheriff's investigation would be wrapped up soon so their special guest could make use of all of the amenities boasted about in recent advertising.

The leather jacket leaned into the back seat and gestured around the property as if confirming this was where they were going to spend their precious time off. Before long, their celebrity guest hopped out and gave him a bear hug, all smiles. Stepping back with one arm still in a half-embrace, he surveyed the grounds, pausing at the view of the open sea. The steady breeze off the water tousled his shoulder-length, dirty blond, straight hair, so he ran fingers through it in a futile effort to tame it.

Something in her abdomen fluttered. It took her back to the concert. It was her senior year of college in New York City. Her roommate had talked her in to going. And she swore he'd worn the same jeans with revealing rips in the thighs that night.

Footsteps on the porch startled her back to the present. Straightening her posture, she made her way toward the foyer in as casual a strut as she could muster with her pup at her side, not expecting him to be the first one through the door. The leather jacket was right behind him.

"Welcome to Pennington Point Inn." She extended her hand. "I'm Elizabeth Pennington."

Pivoting toward her voice, he smiled with sparkling blues and took her hand. His was warm to the touch and firm. She pulled back, careful not to hang on too long.

"Huh-low, Elizabeth." Her name rolled off his tongue like he spoke it often in his luscious Aussie accent. "Pleased tuh meet chew. Eli Hunter."

Amused he'd felt it necessary to introduce himself, she fought to keep her cheeks from revealing how tickled she was but could feel them burning. Grateful the rest of his contingent remained outside, Elizabeth figured they were conducting a security sweep.

"And this is our resident canine, Buddy."

Eli stooped to run a hand across the pup's head. "Ah, good tuh meet chew as well, Buddy."

"We're so pleased you chose the inn for some relaxing time out of your busy schedule. I'm sure you'll find everything you could possibly want during your stay in our newly renovated facilities and, if not, let us know what you need—how we can make it better."

"Sounds great. Oh, and this is Guy." He grabbed the man next to him by the shoulders and shook him playfully. "He's my manager but, more importantly, he keeps me in line. Makes sure I get where I'm supposed to be. . . . *Tries* to keep me out of trouble, but that really takes more than one person to handle."

Guy snorted and nodded once, looking disinterested as he scanned the drawing room over Elizabeth's shoulders.

"Of course, he wasn't so keen on the idea of taking time out of our schedule, but I dragged him anyway. We needed a break."

"I'm sure you'll enjoy it here. They say the salty sea air is a natural relaxant. Even lowers your blood pressure," she offered.

"There you go, Guy," Eli nudged. "Maybe you'll loosen up a bit before we leave."

"Fat chance," he grumbled.

Eager to get their guests settled, Elizabeth focused on check-in.

"Let me get your keys for you."

Navigating around the substantial turned-wood table in the center of the foyer, Elizabeth sized up the floral display, gauging its diminutive stature against the memory of her grandmother's opulent arrangements over the years. Amelia had been proud the flowers were grown in and plucked from her garden on the side of the inn. Elizabeth had plans to resurrect the quarter-acre plot enclosed by a white picket fence, but, at the moment, it would have to wait. Perhaps next spring.

Slipping behind the registration counter, Elizabeth pulled out a small package from the end slot on the desk; a stack of card keys in their individual paper sheaths with a room number written on each. Sliding off the rubber band securing them, she splayed them onto the counter like cards dealt in a poker game.

"I put you and your crew in Moosehead Lodge. It's not the building directly behind this one. It's the one farther out. Take the right fork in the stepping-stone walkway and follow the signs. You will take up all but one of the suites there. I'm afraid that suite won't be opening up like I thought it would. . . . He'll be staying longer than expected," she added, letting her voice trail off. "So for the most part, you'll have privacy there. It should be quiet. And the rooms are on the second floor with great views. Also, for your convenience, the fitness center and spa are located on the first floor in that building." Pushing away images of yellow police tape, she was counting on Deputy Austin to have cleared the area.

"A fitness center. That's great. I need to spend some time in there." Biceps bulging out from under his short sleeves and washboard abs making ripples in his tight tee evidenced consistent time logged with weights, in spite of being on tour.

"Our tennis courts are located down the path next to the garden, and if you're into golf, we run a shuttle over to the local golf course just down the road. But I guess you have your own transportation, don't you?" she conceded. "I also teach an oil painting workshop out on the breakwater near the lighthouse—that is, if the weather and the tide cooperate. And if you're interested in taking any of the boat tours in the area, we can make recommendations for you—"

"No, we're not getting on any boats while we're here, so get that out of your head, Eli," his manager snapped, dismissing it with a swat of his sizable, pudgy hand.

"C'mon, Guy. Where's your sense of adventure?" The world-traveling entertainer seemed genuinely interested in her suggestions, open to exploring the area.

"They're a lot of fun. You can see seals, lighthouses, whales . . . and if you have time, the trip out to Monhegan Island is pretty special," Elizabeth added, not to be foiled by a killjoy. "Just being out on the water is so refreshing."

"No, we're not doing any of that," Guy insisted. "I've got to get you back to the opposite coast in one piece so you can get back into the studio. This trek up here was just supposed to be for some R&R to recover from the tour and get recharged."

"There's always the beach right here," Elizabeth continued. "If you walk straight out the front door and across the lawn, you'll see a break in the line of bushes where you'll find the top of a wooden stairway that will take you down to the beach. It's beautiful there. But if you're looking for something more rigorous, there's the hike through the woods down to the breakwater and out to the lighthouse. I must caution you, though, if the ocean is at all churned up, you really should keep off the breakwater. A rogue wave can come out of nowhere and knock you right off the rocks. And please pass that along to the rest of your group. It can be very dangerous."

"Thanks for the warning. We'll watch our step out there." Eli leaned in, locking eyes with her.

"Damn right, you will. Jesus, Eli. I can't have you going off on any excursions or getting washed out to sea."

Tilting his head in his manager's direction, the country music star winked so only she could see and whispered, "He gets seasick easily."

Elizabeth recalled rumors of her prominent guest's extramarital affairs. "So has your entire party arrived? Will anyone else be joining you?" She was tempted to inquire about his wife but refrained.

"No, this is it. I've got my hands full with these guys as it is," Guy griped. "Don't need anyone else." Snatching the key cards from the counter, he called over his shoulder, "Made the road crew find their own fun. It's going to be long enough as it is."

Elizabeth was counting on it going smoothly for all parties concerned. It had to.

CHAPTER THREE

Elizabeth *heard shuffling* on the sand-covered steps before the brown bob bounced through the front door. She hadn't expected the familiar face to return to the inn, but then again, it was Rashelle. Former assistant manager, former friend. Usually low on cash, often desperate, and always looking for a good time.

"Lizzi, there you are." Her loud, grating voice accentuated her Brooklyn accent. "I knew I'd find you at the ship's wheel. How are you? Great to see you." The bounce in her step was overexaggerated.

With a nagging pang that came from having to confront an undesirable person while remaining calm on the outside, Elizabeth clenched her teeth and took a step forward, folding her arms across her chest while Rashelle continued to gush.

"I *love* how you've redone the place. What a great job. Must have taken forever to do. But, as always, anything you put your touch on comes out gorgeous."

Knowing the answer to her question before she uttered the words, Elizabeth asked it anyway. "Well . . . I certainly didn't expect to see you back here. What do you want?"

"Oh, hey, Liz. Why do I need a reason to stop in to see a friend?"

Could there be any truth that it was simply a social call? Elizabeth knew damn well there wasn't. Ushering her unwelcome visitor into the drawing room to keep their conversation discreet, Elizabeth remained standing even though Rashelle flopped onto the nearest sofa, reupholstered in a smart navy blue broadcloth with white piping. Coordinating beach-themed white toss pillows embroidered with blue shells and crustaceans lined the back of it.

"A friend . . . yeah, I don't think so. Just be honest for once. You're showing up on my doorstep because you need a job."

"What are you talking about? Of course we're friends. We go way back. And friends help each other out."

"Well, all these years, the helping has been very one-sided."

"Lizzi, how can you say—?"

"So what did you do this time to get fired?"

"Who said anything about getting fired?"

"You didn't have to. I know you—all too well."

Rashelle broke eye contact and yanked a pillow onto her lap, fingering the tassel on a corner.

"Ah, Liz. You do know me too well." Her exuberance had evaporated. She continued more softly, as if conceding defeat. "But you gotta know it wasn't my fault."

She was going to take on the role of the victim—again. "Shelle, it never is, is it?"

"C'mon. That's not fair."

"That was a valid assessment, and you know it."

"You haven't heard me out."

"I don't need to."

"What is *up* with you? We're friends. Friends don't turn each other away when they need help."

"We covered that already. We're *not* friends. You had me right where you wanted me for years. Played me for a fool. It took me a while to catch on, but I finally did. We were only 'friends' when it was convenient for you, when it benefited you. There was never any give and take. Just take—from your side. You took advantage of me. And friends *don't* do that."

Elizabeth reflected on their days in college and the times she'd had to rescue Rashelle from the arms—or bed—of a guy with less-than-decent intentions. Time and time again it happened, always after a drinking binge. Although she told herself that was just what friends did for each other, it got old. And when Rashelle came to work at Pennington Point Inn, after Elizabeth stuck her neck out and urged her grandmother to take her on, she'd hoped her co-ed pal had left behind her drinking escapades on the college campus. To her dismay, Rashelle didn't show signs of slowing her imbibing, which influenced the company she kept and the actions she took.

"Liz, I'm sorry if I haven't been the best of friends to you. I'm trying to be, and I'm learning from you. Please, I don't have anyone else to turn to. If there's a shred of decency in your heart, I'm begging for your help. They let me go at the inn up in Boothbay. Said I took some wine from—"

"Did you?"

Tossing the pillow aside by the tassel, Rashelle scooted forward as it tumbled off onto the floor. "Of course not. Why would I do that?" She kept her eyes averted.

Snapping up the pillow and replacing it where it came from, Elizabeth's patience grew thin. "Well then, why would they accuse you of that? Did you try to defend yourself?"

"You *know* I would have defended myself."

Elizabeth could picture Rashelle raising her voice and stomping her foot to make her point; she was never very diplomatic in her negotiations. "So they didn't believe you?"

"No, they said they had security feed that proved otherwise, and they would take it to the police if I didn't leave quietly."

"So did you ask to see it?"

"I—ugh—no, they never would have shown it to me."

Rashelle couldn't have made it more obvious she was guilty. She knew they'd caught her.

At that inopportune moment, Kurt Mitchell, Elizabeth's love interest and recently added business partner, meandered through the foyer. His face lit up when he noticed the girls talking and stepped into the room. "Rashelle, what brings you to this neck of the woods?" Sidling up to Elizabeth, he slipped a loose arm around her waist.

The unemployed drifter perked up and remarked, "Hey, Kurt. Good to see you. We were just talking about where it would make sense to hire me back at the inn."

"Oh, I bet there must be somewhere we can—"

"No, we were *not*." Elizabeth had had her fill of being manipulated.

Kurt read the volatility of the situation and quickly excused himself. "I'll let you two carry on."

"Bye, Kurt," Shelle called after him. "Good to see you." Once he was out of earshot, she whispered, "So you two are together now? How romantic. Playing house, are you?"

"Enough." Elizabeth grabbed her by the arm and pulled her to the front door. "You're not welcome here. How dare you show up and assume you can continue to take advantage of me. You've had too many chances—and second chances—but you don't seem to be able to appreciate them. You can't look any farther than your next drink, can you?"

Rashelle yanked her arm away and scowled.

"There, I said it. You need help, just not the kind of help you were expecting to find here. Get it figured out, Rashelle. Now *go*."

Without another word, the Brooklyn transplant plowed through the door and clomped down the porch steps, letting the screen door slam, not bothering to look back. She carried herself as though she'd exhausted all options and given up.

Elizabeth didn't want to care that Pennington Point Inn had been her last hope. It had taken everything she had to close a door that should have been slammed shut long ago. Was she being overly callous? Was that how it was supposed to end? She'd thrown away a nearly decade-long relationship that began freshman year in the big city when Elizabeth was terrified to be so far from home. Rashelle had befriended her, sharing her campus survival street smarts. Had Elizabeth been keeping some sort of scorecard in her head over the years, and Rashelle had suddenly pulled too far ahead? And now she needed a friend to grab her by the collar and yank her into an AA meeting. *Did Rashelle have anyone in her life who would do that for her?* Sensing someone behind her, she turned to look into Kurt's empathetic face.

"Can imagine how hard that was."

"Yeah." She hated herself for it, fearful he was judging her actions. Feigning a sudden need to attend to the goings on in the kitchen, she turned on her heel and strode toward the dining room.

Kurt remained silent, seeming to understand the wisdom of staying out of a spat between two women. But when Elizabeth reached the threshold, she could still feel his eyes and turned back.

"What's up, Mitchell? Something on your mind?"

"Liz . . ." He closed the distance between them and put a gentle hand on her upper arm. "I hate to pile on more, but I just heard from Sam." She knew what was coming and didn't want to hear the words. "He confirmed the Chase woman's death. They pronounced her on arrival at the hospital. She never regained consciousness."

Suddenly realizing her head had been nodding ever so slightly since he'd touched her arm, she could only utter, "Okay."

"I'm sorry."

"Yeah, me, too." It was hard to wrap her head around the tragedy. From a more practical sense, she wondered about the fallout. *Would the inn be able to recover from it?*

CHAPTER FOUR

The white business-sized envelope was addressed to Elizabeth, not something more general like "Innkeeper" or simply "Pennington Point Inn," and was handwritten. There was a small bulge on one end that slid from side to side when she tilted the envelope. It felt hard and appeared to have a circular shape. There was no return address and the postmark was smudged, but she could make out most of what she recognized as the beginnings of a Maine zip code.

The flap opened easily without tearing as if it had just been sealed. As she pulled out a folded piece of white paper, something metallic fell out and hit the desk below the registration counter, rolling off onto the floor. Slapping the paper onto the surface, Elizabeth pulled out the chair and got down on her hands and knees, groping for the errant insert. Finally her fingers made contact with a woman's ring. Moving it into the light, she took a closer look. It appeared to be a simple engagement ring with a tiny sparkle on top, so small that if it fell out, the wearer wouldn't necessarily notice right away. Snatching the paper off the desk, she began reading the letter written in an unfamiliar script.

Dearest Elizabeth,

As one woman to another, I thought you should know that the man you are cohabitating with, and undoubtedly sharing your bed with, is not the man you think he is. He has a past that I'm certain he hasn't shared with you, one I thought would continue on into a future that included marrying me. I've enclosed the cheap engagement ring he gave me with a promise of a larger one because I no longer have any use for it. If you wouldn't mind, give it back to him for me, ok? Better yet, throw it at him, attached to a sledgehammer.

You know, bad news always travels fast and I found out about you quicker than I cared to. I can't say I don't feel sorry for you. Well, maybe not at first. I was madder than hell when I first found out. I've had some time to get over the initial shock and now I think I do feel sorry for you, now that he's shown what kind of a guy he really is and it's had a chance to sink in. So you can have him. I'm all done trying to salvage our relationship. Take him if you want, but be forewarned. Know what you're getting yourself into. He's a slimy, two-faced, son-of-a-bitch who will just break your heart like he broke mine.

And you might want to watch your back. His previous line of work seems to be coming back to haunt him. The last few times we were together, he thought someone was following him. There have been strange hang-up calls on his cell. And the brakes on my car went out just as I pulled into the garage a couple months ago. Thank God it happened there and not on the highway. I only plowed through the back wall and into the charcoal grill. Could have been so much worse. Coincidence? Could be, but with everything else that was happening, I don't think so.

So I wish you luck. Looks like you'll need it. Oh, and don't lend him any money. It will be the last you'll see of it. He conned me out of a few thousand under the pretense of a *loan to pay for some medical bills (which he wouldn't elaborate about). Who knows, maybe it was for another woman. Ha! He has us all strung out, doesn't he?*

Well, consider yourself warned.

Sincerely,

No longer your competition

Elizabeth's head throbbed. Who could have sent it? Did Kurt have a past he'd kept from her?

She knew he'd been an FBI agent. They'd met when he was sent to Pennington Point for an undercover assignment. But he'd never mentioned being engaged or seriously seeing anyone. By the end of his Maine assignment, she and Kurt had made a connection—one she'd hoped would develop into a meaningful relationship, and she'd thought he felt the same. However, they went their separate ways, and she didn't hear from him again for almost a year before he tracked her down at her design office in Connecticut. In spite of his evasiveness when she inquired of his whereabouts since she'd last seen him—owing to the fact he couldn't discuss his work for security reasons—they reconnected and maintained a long-distance relationship while he took on various assignments around the country. When he grumbled about having to travel so much and how he hated being away from her, she took a risk and asked if he'd like to join her in running the inn. It wasn't to be a financial investment on his part. She'd already taken out construction loans with the property as collateral, but she was hoping he would agree to share the burden of day-to-day operations, allowing them more time together. Of course, it could be the ultimate test of a relationship—going from rarely seeing each other to spending every day dealing with the stresses of running a business. It hadn't taken him long to consider her offer; and by the time he'd wrapped up his ties at the Bureau and trained his replacement, Kurt joined her a couple months before the inn's grand reopening date.

With letter in hand, she wondered what other questions she should have asked him. What else in his past didn't she know about?

CHAPTER FIVE

The room was mournfully quiet except for an unnatural buzz that rang in her ears. It didn't appear as though anyone had used the equipment since the poor woman's accident a couple days earlier. Yellow police tape that had cordoned off the area had been removed at Elizabeth's urging after a scant twenty-four hours, but had the damage been done and scared guests away? There was nothing to hint at the tragedy that had unfolded on the bench press, yet sadness resonated through her. Lost in her concern over the effect the incident would have on the inn's reputation, she hadn't heard footfalls in the carpeted hall and jolted at the voice behind her.

"Quite a nice setup you've got." Eli's down-under inflection sounded delightful to her ears.

Elizabeth spun around to look into the face of their most famous guest. She caught her breath and struggled to pull her thoughts back to what his needs were. After all, each guest had his own agenda, and that needed to be the focus of management and staff.

"We're quite proud of the new facilities," she announced. "Have you had a chance to try out the equipment yet?"

"Naw, we've been quite lazy so far." He stepped closer as he confessed his transgressions that, in the grand scheme of things, bordered on trivial.

She was amused he'd used the word "we," as if he could blame his lack of exercise on the entire group. *Whatever helps you to sleep at night, love.*

"I think our tour wiped us out more than we realized." He searched her face as if to verify he could confide in her. "Ya know, we're not twenty-something anymore, so we need to guard our time . . . our health . . . our emotional well-being." His clenched teeth told there was more to it than he was willing to share.

"Yeah, that makes sense." She wanted to be a sounding board to support him, yet grew uncomfortable as he inched closer, whiskey on his breath.

As he slid his hand around her shoulders, her body stiffened. Incredulous that this was happening with a megastar in the fitness center of her family's inn, she endeavored to remain cool while he rambled.

"God, Elizabeth, you've got the most enchanting eyes." He latched on to her forearm, his accent dripping Aussie. "You pulled me in. . . . I'm not supposed to be attracted to anyone else, but you're absolutely beautiful. Tell me you'll come back to my room with me. We'll just talk. I've got wine. Do you like wine? Red or white? It doesn't matter; I've got both. Or maybe you're partial to tequila . . . or rum. I've got a smooth coconut rum. It's amazing over ice."

Elizabeth was stunned to hear him slur his words, yet she felt the pull of his charisma and fought the urge to follow him back to his room. She reasoned she should at least escort him to make sure he didn't wander off and put himself in danger—like from the obvious threats of the cross-our-fingers-it-will-be-adequate row of boxwoods along the edge of the precipice, planted long ago to keep guests from doing anything stupid, and the perilous hike down the steep trail to the breakwater. Surely he wouldn't be heading out in the dark. Or would he? Where was the rest of his group? He had a single room so it was entirely possible they weren't aware he was out and about, feeling no pain, a detriment to himself. Her thoughts drifted back to the boxwoods. It was times like this she questioned their adequacy, but the unobscured view always took priority. She prayed she wouldn't regret that decision at some point in the future.

"All right, Mr. Hunter. Let's head up to your room."

"Awesome. I'd love some company. It's a bit lonely. The band seems to do their own thing, and Guy . . . well, I don't know what Guy's doing. He always seems to be busy."

"Let's get you back upstairs so you can relax, which is why you came here, right?"

"Absolutely." His arm found its way down around her waist, and she responded in kind. "Ya know, my first name is really Hunter."

"It is?" She thought it best to keep him talking.

"Yeah, my original manager thought Eli Hunter sounded more country."

"I think he was right."

"It's tough enough to get people to take you seriously as a country singer when you have an Australian accent. You've at least got to have a name that fits."

"Makes sense to me." She kept him moving forward.

The two wobbled in their attempt to walk in sync up the stairs and down the hall, bumping into the wall every few steps. He fumbled with his card key, so she slipped it from his fingers and slid it into the slot. The green light appeared, and she pushed open the door.

"Oh, here we are." He sounded surprised he'd found his way back yet quickly settled into the familiar surroundings and made his way to the wet bar. "What can I get you, Elizabeth?" He already had a wine glass in hand and retrieved a bottle of white out of the mini-fridge.

Out of deference to her celebrity guest, she restrained herself from laughing out loud. How did he know what kind of wine she liked? Or that she liked wine at all? Had to be a coincidence. He was simply making an assumption based on all the women he'd known. Nevertheless, she was drawn in. Her loins tingled uncontrollably, and she had no intention of reining in the stimulation. It was all in the name of keeping guests happy . . . and safe. After all, how many women could say they'd been entertained by one of their favorite country singers? Of course, she couldn't very well tell anyone. Still, it would be exciting to have it as her secret. But what would Kurt say? Where was he at the moment? Waiting for her in front of the fireplace with two glasses of Cabernet—his favorite wine? Would he ever figure out she really preferred white? She wasn't particularly picky about what kind, as long as it was dry. Maybe she'd hint around about it tonight. At least she didn't have to worry about red warming to room temperature and becoming less palatable. She wouldn't stay long. She'd catch up with Kurt soon.

"White wine would be lovely. Thank you." The tingling had spread throughout her body. Her fingertips began to perspire. They locked eyes when he handed her the glass, overfilled and nearly sloshing above the rim. He scooped up a short, stout glass with a trace of amber liquid in it. Grabbing a bottle from the counter, he splashed more out than in, but enough to bring the level to half full. Plunking down the bottle, he left the cap where it lay and swung around toward her with his glass on a collision course with hers. She pulled back to soften the blow and prevent breakage, allowing a soft clink.

"Cheers, Elizabeth." His accent was luscious. She loved how her name slipped easily off his tongue, but she hated how guilty she felt being with another man. Assuring herself it was all very innocent, she knew Kurt would feel otherwise if he knew.

"Cheers, Eli."

"Please call me Hunter."

"Okay." If anything, she should be calling him Mr. Hunter and should never have agreed to have a drink with him. Her attempts to convince herself she was merely being an attentive innkeeper were failing miserably.

"Here's to this lovely New England inn of yours. Ya know, I'll have to admit I wasn't so keen on the idea of coming all the way up here, but Guy insisted it would be a welcome respite after a grueling schedule. I think he's right. Just what we needed."

"Glad you think so."

"At first I thought he was kidding." He gave her a playful swat on the shoulder.

"So it was your manager's idea to come to Pennington Point, not yours?" She recalled the conversation in the lobby upon his arrival. It sounded then that Hunter had been the one to suggest it.

"Yeah, I don't know him all that well, so I couldn't read him. But once I realized he was serious, I told him we needed to make it a proper holiday and stay for at least three weeks."

"Oh, he's fairly new to you?"

"Yeah, I picked him up a few months before this tour." He turned sullen. "I miss Chappy. . . . Hard to replace someone like that, but I think Guy will work out just fine."

"What happened?" She was almost afraid to ask.

Throwing back the whiskey, he became quiet. "He got sick and had to step away for a while and focus on his health. He couldn't handle the grueling schedule."

"So sorry to hear."

"Yeah, I hope he's able to beat this. He was more than a manager to me. We'd been together from almost the beginning." He retreated to the bar to pour another splash before returning to her side.

They locked eyes again, and she averted hers, struggling to keep from getting drawn in. She suddenly felt the warmth of his hand in hers. He pulled her toward the expansive bed in the middle of the room.

"Hunter, no."

He stopped short and teetered back. They stood as close as two people could without making contact.

"What are you—I can't. Please."

"What's wrong, Elizabeth? I thought I could feel something between us. Tell me I'm wrong."

God, she knew he was right, but she couldn't admit it. "I have to go. This isn't right. . . . As much as I'd like to stay, this is wrong on so many levels."

She plunked her glass on the counter before heading to the door. He was right behind her. She spun around to cut him off. Placing her palm on his chest, she could feel his heart pounding against his rib cage and the warmth of his skin through the shirt.

"Why don't you get some rest. I think you could use it. Let's have breakfast in the morning. How does that sound?"

He pouted like a spoiled child but perked up at the idea of seeing her again. *Why did his eyes have to be so damn blue?*

"All right, I'll see you in the morning."

Elizabeth placed a gentle kiss on his cheek and slipped out of his room, grateful the hall was empty. She knew they wouldn't be getting together for breakfast. He wouldn't remember much from their evening encounter. She depended on it.

CHAPTER SIX

S*am skipped up the* front porch stairs with an urgency in his step and burst through the door. Striding across the foyer, he started in before he'd reached the registration desk.

"Elizabeth, I'm afraid I'm going to have to have a little chat with the grieving husband."

It didn't sound like he planned to offer his condolences. "What's up? I thought you were going to say he was free to go home and bury his wife."

"Something cropped up during the autopsy that ran contradictory to the rest of the findings. I want to be sure we got the facts straight when we spoke to him initially."

"What was it?"

He gave her that look that she should know better than to ask.

"Come on, Sam. This is my place. As I've said before, I've got a huge responsibility to maintain the safety of my guests."

"I really don't think you've got anything to worry about. I just need to follow through and check something out."

Elizabeth didn't take any comfort from his assurances but knew there was no point in pursuing it further. He'd learned the job from his father, who was a stickler for the rules. Perhaps the deputy was even more so. She had to give him credit for taking his responsibility seriously. She also needed to find out what his suspicions were. Could troubles be starting up at Pennington Point again? The inn couldn't afford more bad press.

On Sam's way out the door, he held it open for Kurt, and they exchanged brief pleasantries.

Elizabeth saw the wrinkles on Kurt's forehead long before he reached the front desk. He strode across the lobby and whacked the edge of the counter with a stack of mail, startling her.

"What's that?" The envelopes were yellowed and water-stained—looked like a couple dozen—one of which toppled from the counter to the desk below.

"It's mail." His tone was flat and thick with condescendence.

"I can see that," she pushed back, glancing at the errant piece to confirm it, in fact, belonged to the inn. "Where did you get it? . . . And why does it look this way?"

"I imagine it looks this way because it sat in the mailbox for a long time, waiting to be picked up."

"What mailbox? The mailman brings the mail in and drops it off and picks up whatever outgoing mail we have."

"Since the inn opened, yes. But while it was closed, he had nowhere else to put it but in the box at the end of the access road. And it was jammed pretty tight in there."

38

"There's a mailbox that belongs to the inn? I never knew we had one."

"Apparently we do." He didn't try to hide his discontent. "It's completely overgrown—I almost didn't see it; it's all rusty, and the flag has fallen off. The door was tough to open."

She started to paw through the mail, pulling aside the junk pieces and tossing them. How long had they sat there? Had she missed an important bill or notice? She snatched a breath when she reached one that had a red stamped message on the outside: FINAL NOTICE.

Leaning in, Kurt grabbed the envelope off the counter. "What the hell!" His voice was louder than she would have liked. "Elizabeth, this is the town of Pennington Point. Have you not been paying the property taxes?"

"Property taxes?"

"This can't be happening. How could you let this—"

"Kurt, I had no idea. I thought they got paid when you made your mortgage payment. They're included in my monthly payment on my Connecticut condo."

"You don't *have* a mortgage on his place."

"Exactly."

"So you have to pay them on your own. It's not a finite amount that gets prorated over the life of your mortgage, and then you're done. You always have to pay taxes on your property."

"Oh Kurt, I'm terrible at the business side of things. I didn't realize there were bills to pay on a property that had been in my family for years and was practically destroyed by a hurricane. I knew my grandmother owned it outright. And we'd turned off the power and water. What could possibly be left? It didn't dawn on me there was anything to pay besides insurance." The words sounded ridiculous spilling out of her mouth, but she had to put up some sort of defense, feeble as it was.

Snatching the envelope back from him, she slid a finger under the edge of the flap and eased it open, pulling out the letter. Her eyes darted back and forth across the page, yet she couldn't make sense of the words. Returning to the subject, she picked up on the word "lien."

"Oh my God, they're putting a lien on the property."

"They may already have, depending on the date of that letter. *Damn it*, Liz."

"How can they do that? I never received the bills." What had she done? Her grandmother would be so disappointed in her. Was she going to lose the inn? Her childhood home?

"It's not like you left a forwarding address. Hell, look how long it took me to find you, and that's what I'm trained to do." His voice thundered to a crescendo before dropping off.

Buddy growled softly from under the desk, and she shushed him.

"If you don't pay your taxes—" He scattered the envelopes across the counter. "—and it looks like they made several attempts to reach you—they have every right to do that. You owe them money and haven't responded to any of their notifications. It appears to them that you have no intention of paying. They can take possession of the property and sell it off to get what you owe them."

"But the inn and the land would be worth so much more than what I could possibly owe. How can they do that?"

"With the funds from auctioning off the place, they would take what they're owed, and after any other creditors are paid off, you would get what's left over."

"Oh, dear God. We can't lose this place . . . and after all the money we've spent to fix it up."

"It's certainly a possibility—depending on how far they are in the process."

"Okay . . . I'll, uh . . . I'll look into it." She had no clue where to start to unravel the mess she'd inadvertently gotten them into. And he could tell.

"Give them to me. I'll see what I can find out." He glanced at his watch. "They're closed now. I'll head into town in the morning." He didn't make eye contact with her as he gathered the half dozen or so envelopes with the same red stamp on the front and disappeared back through the front door.

Although she'd heard it a million times, the screen door slamming shut seemed louder than usual and gave her a jolt. She'd have to ask him about the mysterious letter another time.

CHAPTER SEVEN

Elizabeth *found herself* in territory her grandmother would not only have been a regular visitor to but confident in as well. She wasn't sure how to put into words she was sorry his wife had passed away. Not only passed away. She'd suffered a horrific death from dropping a staggering fifty-pound barbell on her throat. Her neck had snapped in what the EMTs estimated was a relatively quick death. The full autopsy results were still pending.

How do you attempt to provide comfort in that situation?

Gazing out to the open sea, as if looking for answers, his back was to Elizabeth. She regarded how close he was to the row of boxwoods planted along the cliff.

As the ambassador of the inn, she felt the need to connect with him—at least offer whatever he might need to get though his ordeal, no matter how uncomfortable she felt.

"Mr. Chase?" She was struck by his strong build. A good-looking man, relatively young, probably early thirties. His recently deceased wife, perhaps a little younger. Their hopes and dreams for a future together had been dashed in one swift, deadly slip. She wondered if he replayed that morning in his head, over and over, wishing he'd gone with her to spot her during the workout.

For a moment, he remained steady on his spot as if he hadn't heard her. She opened her mouth and took a couple steps closer to try again but held up.

As he turned toward her, his eyes looked hollow, like they were far away and could see straight through her. She shook off a shiver.

"Mr. Chase, I wanted to tell you, on behalf of the entire staff of the inn, how sorry we are about your wife." The words felt awkward, but she hoped their good intentions were accepted.

There was no flicker of acknowledgment. Instead, his gaze remained fixed on the ground between them.

Elizabeth was touched by the sadness he carried. Her instincts told her to hug him, but she struggled with what was appropriate in her role.

"Please let us know whatever you need. We are sincerely sorry for your loss."

He glanced up and made a connection with her. "I appreciate your gesture. . . . There is nothing you or anyone else can do at this point. What's done is done." His words plodded in a strangely staccato rhythm as if they were rehearsed. His breathing grew labored.

He backed up to the hedge, terrifyingly close. Elizabeth took in a breath.

She offered again, "I'm so sorry."

"There's nothing else that can be done," he repeated and took another step away. "No turning back."

"Please, don't get too close to the edge." The words caught in her throat.

He chuckled, sounding oddly condescending under the circumstances. "I'm fine. Really." He took another step back.

Lunging forward, she grabbed his arm and yanked him away from the cliff. In the awkward moment that ensued, they spun around together, landing hard on the ground with her on top of him.

"Oh my God. That wasn't supposed to happen. I'm so sorry." Elizabeth was mortified to be straddling a guest's waist, her face inches from his.

He drew in a couple of ragged breaths but didn't utter a word.

Elizabeth tried again. "I'm so sorry." As she hovered above him, her cheeks started to burn. Who had witnessed her embarrassing blunder?

He wiggled out from beneath her and crawled a few feet away before turning back. "You'll never understand. Don't even try." Scrambling to his feet, he added, "You're very sweet, Elizabeth. . . . Who knows, maybe you and I would have had a chance in another lifetime. Unfortunately, this is what we've been dealt in this one."

She watched in horror as he dashed for the bushes and dove over them, sailing into the air in a swan dive and then disappeared below her line of sight. Then came a soft thud.

What had she done? Had she pushed him too far in her attempt to console him?

She ran to the hedges and peered over the side. He hadn't gotten very far. He lay sprawled on the wooden stairway with his arms and legs splayed in awkward angles, two tiers down to the beach below, bloody and lifeless. Elizabeth shrieked and ran to the top of the stairs, hoping he wasn't another unfortunate victim at Pennington Point Inn. She grabbed her phone and dialed 9-1-1. *Please, Lord, let him be all right.*

CHAPTER EIGHT

The slam of the screen door announced the arrival of a longtime regular guest of the pre-hurricane inn. Elizabeth wrapped up her call and got to her feet in as much a defensive move as in deference to the old woman's loyalty.

"Mrs. Leibowitz, so good to see you." Her voice sounded odd to her ears as she feigned cheerfulness. How her grandmother was able to greet each and every guest with a warm, seemingly genuine welcome was beyond Elizabeth and something she hadn't perfected yet. Not even close. And this guest was not welcome in her book. During her last visit, Elizabeth had caught the feisty old woman using the tunnels to pilfer bottles from the wine cellar. Always demanding and unreasonable, her name had been purposely left off the mailing list for the reopening announcement. "Welcome back to Pennington Point Inn. What brings you here?"

As the short, bushy-browed, silver-haired woman leaned away from Elizabeth and shot her a perplexed look, her loose jowls jiggled.

"What do you mean, what brings me here?" Her voice was more grating than Lizzi remembered. "For God's sake, this is my usual week. I always stay here this week of the summer. You know that. Well, at least your grandmother would have remembered that." She wagged a crooked forefinger at her. The lines encircling her lips gave her the look of perpetually sucking on a cigarette.

Elizabeth knew there was no usual week, but with Mrs. L, there was no reasoning with her. "Of course, and did you make a reservation? I don't recall seeing it."

"A reservation? You've *got* to be kidding me. I *told* you I come every year at same time. You know that. Or you *should* know that. And it's always the same room. The end unit in Acadia. I'm dying to see how you've redecorated it. You know, it took you entirely too long to fix up the place and get it open again. That was pretty annoying. It's not like you're on an island where everything has to be brought in. I mean—*two years*—what took you so long? Good God, the world was created in seven days."

Elizabeth let her comments about the extended delay go unanswered. "Mrs. Leibowitz, I'm sorry we didn't have a standing reservation for you. And you're right, my grandmother would have known exactly when you were arriving, but I'm running the inn now and doing the best I can. As I'm sure you can imagine, it's been a little hectic getting the extensive renovations done in time for the reopening. Parts of Acadia aren't quite finished, and I'm afraid your usual room is one of the ones that still need completing."

"*Are you kidding me?* What the *hell* have you been doing all this time? *My* room isn't ready? Well how long do you think it will be? I'll just grab a drink in the bar while I'm waiting—on the house, of course."

"No, Mrs. Leibowitz, you don't understand—"

"No, honey, *you* don't understand. When you don't have a guest's room ready—especially such a loyal guest like me—you need to make reparations. A simple drink is the least you can do." She turned on her heel, leaving a tote on the floor below the counter, and took a couple steps toward the darkened room with overturned chairs on the tables. "What the—"

"I'm sorry, Mrs. Leibowitz, the bar doesn't open until five o'clock."

"For the love of God, why not?" She lunged toward the front desk, latching on to the edge of the counter as if she'd been parched for days, and Elizabeth was depriving her of drinking water.

"We found that no one was using it until later in the day, so it didn't make sense for us to staff it throughout—"

"Well, *I* do, and that should be all the justification you need," she thundered, sliding her gnarled fingers from the marble top.

Elizabeth paused to allow her words to echo through the foyer, giving her the chance to hear how pompous she sounded, doubting she noticed. "We'll certainly take it under advisement. But right now you need to understand the situation with your room. It's not that housekeeping hasn't made it up yet, it isn't finished from a construction standpoint. If you were to walk in the front door, you'd be able to see through to the back. It's just two-by-fours. The sheet rockers still need to get in there. And there's only a subfloor. Still a lot of work to be done."

The ornery woman glared but held her tongue. Elizabeth grabbed the opportunity to jump in and continue with her train of thought. "But I'm sure we'll be able to find something just as lovely for you." Her fingers danced across the keyboard in search of an unassigned room to appease their disgruntled guest.

"Well, what do you have for me?" As she smacked the counter with the palm of her hand, Elizabeth jolted. Patience was not something anyone could accuse Mrs. L of having.

Scrolling through all the reservations, matching confirmed arrivals against the list of available rooms, she came up empty. Due to the construction delays, there simply weren't any rooms. Where could she put her? Elizabeth glanced up and caught the old woman's icy stare. *Should she?* "Give me a minute. I need to check on something."

"Well, hurry it up already. I've waited long enough as it is," she grumbled. "For God's sake, your grandmother ran the place better than this—on a bad day."

Sliding her cell from her pocket, Elizabeth stepped away from earshot and dialed Kurt. After a couple rings he picked up. "Yeah, Liz, what's up?"

Cupping her hand around her mouth, she asked, "Hey, can you tell me if room 301 is available yet? Have they cleared it?"

"Yeah, as a matter of fact they just took down the police tape. Why?"

"I need to put someone in there."

"Really? How'd that happen? Wasn't the whole building originally reserved by the touring entourage?"

"Yeah, but I have a walk-in. A *special* walk-in. I'll fill you in when I see you."

"Okay, but it will need to be made up. Would you like me to have someone from housekeeping take care of that ASAP?"

She pivoted so her guest could hear. "That's terrific. Thanks so much for going out of your way to make that possible. Yes, I know she'll appreciate that. Who wouldn't? It's such a gorgeous room and a great location. The view is to die for." It hit her that her last comment was in poor taste, but it had slipped out before she could prevent it. And it was between the two of them.

"Uh . . . if you say so."

"Sorry. I'll catch up with you later. Thanks again. I appreciate it. Owe you one."

Dismissing Kurt, she turned to Mrs. Leibowitz and informed her it would be half an hour to forty-five minutes while house-keeping changed out a room that a guest had just vacated. In the meantime, she could make herself comfortable in the drawing room. Elizabeth would talk to the wine steward about running out a glass for her to enjoy while she waited.

Sputtering, the elderly woman tottered over to the same sofa Rashelle had selected—the one closest to the door—and flopped her sizable mass onto it, sending a pillow on each side of her tumbling to the floor. Elizabeth grimaced, regretting her choice of white pillows.

"Make it a Chianti," she barked. "A nice dry one. And make sure they select a *good* year. God, I certainly hope you have a better handle on which vintages to steer clear of than the previous administration."

Elizabeth straightened up and felt her back tighten. *No one* was going to speak ill of the "previous administration"—certainly not of her grandmother or the infallible Chef Tony. Before she could lash out with a retort, she could hear Amelia inside her head assuring her it was all right and to let it go. Acquiescing, she released a protracted but silent breath.

She didn't have long to dwell on the derogatory remark before another guest burst through the front door, this one with a cat carrier in tow and a booming nasally voice that sounded like he had a fistful of gravel caught in his throat.

"Hello, hello. Wow, *that* was a longer drive than I anticipated," he whined as he plodded across the foyer, bumping the cat box into the table, sending the vase teetering precariously close to toppling. Elizabeth lunged for the office door but pulled back when the flowers stopped wobbling. "Man, I thought we were *never* going to get here." He cleared his throat with a flourish meant for getting a concert hall's attention. "Geez, you really should put in the brochure how long the road to the inn is, too. I thought we were lost for sure. Heh, heh." He was clearly amused by his humor.

Struggling to maintain a welcoming smile, Elizabeth observed the cat's face peering out of the carrier, its beady eyes darting to assess its new surroundings. Buddy stirred at her feet, perhaps sensing the feline. Could also have been the smell emanating from its owner, a mix of perspiration, cigarette smoke, and cheap cologne that grew overpowering when he reached the desk. He plunked down the box on the counter, and Elizabeth did her best to keep her expression even. None of her design clients had ever made her regret having to take her next breath. Her smokestack designer boss, yes. Clients, no.

"I see you've brought a friend." She nodded toward the weathered box with scuffed up corners.

"Oh, *yes*. We go *everywhere* together. Haven't been separated since I rescued her." He seemed proud of that fact and probably saw no reason not to share it with everyone.

As Mrs. L perked up on the couch mere feet away, Elizabeth cringed she hadn't had a chance to put a call in to the kitchen to order the glass of wine yet. The cat man carried on, oblivious to her distress.

"This is Boots. I named her that because she has white on all four of her little feet that is just so cute." Some pet owners thought everyone should be in love with their furry kids. And this one never considered cats might not be allowed at the inn. Had she made a mistake including Buddy in the advertising? She'd meant for it to imply warm, inviting lodging, not a free-for-all for everyone to bring their pets. She'd have to reconsider the promotional materials when she had a moment.

To Elizabeth's dismay, Mrs. L scooted her large rear end off the sofa and wobbled back into the lobby. "Did I hear you say your cat's name is Boots?"

The middle-aged man beamed at the attention and rotated the carrier around so she could see the cat's face. "Yes, that's right. There she is. Isn't she a beauty?"

"Oh, she's just *precious*. You know, I used to have a Maine Coon cat that I'd named Boots. Isn't that a coincidence?"

"Wow, really? Maybe my Boots is a reincarnation of your Boots. Wouldn't *that* be interesting."

As the two engaged in a lively discussion about their cats, Elizabeth grabbed the opportunity to phone the kitchen and put a rush on the Chianti. Before long, one of the waitstaff arrived with glass in hand, which was met with, "Well, there you are. *That* didn't need to take so long." Mrs. L glanced at the inn's newest arrival. "You know, I've been coming here for years, and the service now leaves a lot to be desired. You might want to reconsider before you actually check in. First, they don't have my reservation. Then, they don't have my room ready. And then they make me wait for the glass of wine they offered to make me feel better about screwing up in the first place."

The young waiter shot a puzzled look to Elizabeth, who dismissed the old woman's crass remarks with an almost indiscernible shake of her head. "Thank you, Robby. I appreciate you taking care of that so quickly."

In awe of the simple gesture, the cat man's brows nearly reached his receding hairline. "How nice is *that* to be greeted with a glass of wine at check-in." He turned to the waiter and ordered a glass of Riesling. "That's great. Thank you so much. That will taste great after the long drive." Poking his face into the carrier, nose-to-nose with his feline, he assured her they would get her fresh water, too.

Robby, again, looked for guidance from his boss who clenched her jaw and nodded.

Mrs. L wedged her way between the man and the carrier to fuss over the cat who let out a yowl, startled by the stranger in her face. Buddy jumped to his feet from under the counter and let out a sharp woof, further provoking the cat who hissed, thumping so hard against the side of the box, it shook. Elizabeth grabbed her pup's collar and scolded him, ordering him back down on the floor. He complied, but his eyes told her he wasn't at all happy about it.

The man lunged toward the cat and tried to soothe her but then turned on the innkeeper. "What was *that*? My God, that came out of nowhere. Is that supposed to be the sweet pup that 'welcomes each and every guest like they're family'? *Geez.* That's just not right."

The sound of his unnecessarily loud voice thumping through her head with every syllable brought on the fringes of a tension headache. The situation was reeling out of Elizabeth's control, and she needed to get her hands back on the reins.

"Why don't we get you checked into your room. I'm sure your Riesling will be along soon."

For a fleeting moment, Elizabeth wondered if she'd made a mistake by turning away Rashelle. Even though they weren't friends, at least she knew how to run the front desk. Her college roommate also knew how to smile convincingly and put up with all the unexpected crap guests dished out. Elizabeth had hoped she'd get better at it, but the last two had tested her limits. Now she'd have to ask housekeeping to go above and beyond to clean the cat man's room when he checked out, so the next guest to check in with pet dander allergies wouldn't have an issue. She would definitely have to revisit the promotional materials, but at the moment she couldn't spare the time to rework them or the cost to reprint them. They would have to do for now.

As the cat man headed off to his room with his furry companion in tow, her cell vibrated in her pocket. Elizabeth could hear the deputy speaking on the other end of the line but wrestled with the words to make sense of them.

"They found *what* when they were bulldozing?" Yet another construction delay was in the making. Throbbing at her temples threatened to creep to the back of her head.

"Let me start at the beginning. The crew chief told me after they'd cleared the trees in the area where the additional tennis courts are going, they brought in a bulldozer to smooth out the surface and dig down to the depth they need to layer in the materials. They ran into a little snag."

"A *little* snag? How little—or should I ask how big? For God's sake, Sam, I don't know how much more bad news I can handle. What did they find?"

"It looks like there's going to be somewhat of a delay while they wait for state police forensics to take a look. Who knows, maybe it's animal bones and—"

"Animal bones? They found bones? But they might be human?"

"Uhh . . . we don't know that yet. Forensics will take a look first and determine exactly what was unearthed."

"Depending on the age, whether it's animal or human, we might be talking about a full-fledged archeological dig or a crime scene investigation. That could take—" She didn't have it in her to attach a time frame. "Oh, Lord. Keep me up to date on the progress." The one saving grace she could come up with was they'd decided to do the project in two phases and not bulldoze the existing courts. Though they were in sore need of resurfacing,

at least guests had two courts to play on while the new construction dragged on.

"And, Sam."

"Yeah."

"Any word on Mr. Chase's condition?"

"Last I heard, he was still critical."

"I see."

"I don't want to offer you any false words of encouragement,
Liz."

"I appreciate that. . . . Let me know if anything changes."
Praying the poor man would fully recover, she tried to maintain
positive thoughts for him and his family, and also for the inn and
her family's reputation.

"Sure thing." The deputy signed off.

CHAPTER NINE

When the head chef showed up for his first day of work, he didn't resemble what one would picture as a chef, but in all fairness there really wasn't a stereotype for the vocation. Clearly vexed when Elizabeth had to remind him to pull his hair back into a ponytail, Vincenzo tried to draw the line at wearing a chef's hat. He also made sure it was clear *no one* could call him Vinny. She imagined that included his mother, if she were alive.

In spite of the weeks that had passed since his arrival and tumultuous start, she still hadn't clicked with him like she had with the rest of her staff, each one meticulously selected from the pool of applicants to serve as ambassadors for the inn that had been in the Pennington family for three generations. She'd hoped they would have developed more of a rapport. Instead, she endured an ongoing nagging perception he resented her intrusions into the kitchen and occasional menu tweaks. He was going to have to learn how to leave his ego out of it, or his future at the inn would be bleak.

Squeaky hinges announced her arrival as she poked her head just past the half-open door. Vincenzo looked up from the chopping block, his white toque perched cockeyed on his head as if he knew she was on her way and plopped it there for her benefit.

"Sup?"

Sup? He certainly wouldn't have addressed her grandmother that way. She needed to work on demanding more respect from him.

"Before the lunch rush, I wonder if you'd have a moment to chat."

"What about?"

She took a couple steps in and let the door swing shut. "Clambakes." The word brought a smile to her face. "They used to be a cherished tradition here at the inn—the guests loved them—and I'd like to bring them back. They're complicated to pull off, but—"

"*I* know how to do a clambake."

Aware her expression undoubtedly conveyed her disbelief, she thought back to his résumé to dredge up a previous work experience where he would have had the opportunity to do a clambake. His most recent and longest stint was at a major hotel on the Las Vegas Strip. The nearest ocean was hundreds of miles away.

"You do?"

"Sure, it's not hard."

"Well, there's a lot of prep work, and everything you would need has to be lugged down to the beach and—"

"I know that. You don't have to tell me."

Feeling her face growing red and a lightheadedness threatening to strike down her projected authority, she took a moment to pull in air and let it out again without making a sound.

"Why do I get the feeling you don't want me to interfere with how you run this kitchen?" she asked slowly and deliberately.

"Because there's no need to. I know what I'm doing. You saw my résumé. You know my background. And you should know I can handle this little kitchen with no problem."

Little kitchen? It might be smaller than his previous work environment, but no less important.

Elizabeth gave her head a tilt to let him know she'd caught his dig. "That may be. But I am your boss and this is *my* inn. I *will* be involved with how this kitchen is run, whether you like it or not. So if you have a problem with that, then you have a problem with me. And that won't be tolerated."

"Well, if you can't see where I'm coming from, you won't have a chef to run *your* little kitchen."

"Is this really where you want to take this conversation?" Horrified to have pushed it that far, suddenly she could feel herself backpedaling. She couldn't lose her chef, and he knew it.

"I'm not taking it anywhere. We need to reach an understanding so we can work together. . . . Look, I guess I'm not used to having someone looking over my shoulder all the time. I like working independently and thought that's what it would be like here."

Elizabeth couldn't imagine *any* work environment, especially in the hospitality industry, where one could work alone, unimpeded. She also couldn't afford him walking out, no matter how obnoxious and pretentious he was. Otherwise, she'd be donning an apron and flipping burgers for dinner and pancakes in the morning.

"Well, perhaps it was a bit premature of me to introduce the idea of clambakes. We'll hold off on them for now and at some point down the road, we'll revisit the idea."

"No, we don't need to do that. I can handle it." His words grew louder.

She remained calm on the outside, keeping her voice steady. "No, it would be best to let you get your bearings in a new place and do your best work from the kitchen." She restrained herself from using the word "little" to describe it. "Show me what you can do in here, and then we can branch out from there."

Leaving the chef with the not-so-subtle message she was in charge, and he needed to prove to her he deserved to be in her kitchen, she slipped back out though the exit side of the swinging doors, the side that didn't squeak. She could only pray his previous employer wasn't trying to lure him back.

CHAPTER TEN

The *fluorescent yellow flyer* caught her attention before she reached the bottom of the stairs in search of her first cup of coffee. It hung next to the door out to the front porch. As she got closer, she could make out: BACK BY POPULAR DEMAND, CLAMBAKE ON THE BEACH. Her back stiffened. "Oh no, he didn't." This chef was going to be trouble. "He got here earlier than usual this morning," she mumbled.

The neon signs were plastered all over the first floor. Next to the front desk, on either side of the sitting room fireplace, on the mirror behind the bar, and next to the doorway out to the back porch. One by one she gathered them, gently pulling clear cellophane tape off freshly painted walls, cringing until she could verify the latex hadn't come off with each tug.

With the stack of flyers clutched in one hand, she headed to the kitchen but stopped short of entering. If Vincenzo was going to test her, she'd provide him with his own test. They would see if the cocky know-it-all could pull off a traditional New England clam-bake. She doubted he could. Maybe she would make it interesting and invite the *Portland Herald* food critic. Was Elizabeth willing to let him flop? Run the risk of tarnishing the inn's reputation? She wouldn't need to. She'd let him get to the point where he had to admit defeat and ask for help. Then she'd send in reinforcements and save the day.

Shoving the swinging door harder than necessary, she popped into the kitchen as Vincenzo washed a large pot in the sink on the far wall. Several more dirty pans were lined up to the side. He didn't appear to hear her enter in spite of the creak of the door. She waited for him to finish. As he turned to flip the pot over to drain on the counter, he caught her in his peripheral and abandoned his task for a moment.

Grabbing a corner of his white apron, he dried his hands as he sized up his adversary. "Good morning, Miss Pennington." Elizabeth was glad his tone was even and not instigative.

"Good morning, Vincenzo." She raised her flyer-filled fist. "I see you've decided to go ahead with the clambake after all."

"You took them all down?" His voice boomed in the small space.

"Oh, no. Not all of them. There are still plenty for the guests to learn of your venture. I thought I would whittle the number down so it would be more tasteful. I'll admit I was surprised to see them, but then I realized this could be a real opportunity you've created for the inn. I just got off the phone with the food critic at the *Portland Herald,* and she said she'd love to stop by and partake of the event and write a review for us." Fibbing didn't come easily to her. She struggled not to blink more often than was natural but was unsure what that felt like at the moment.

His right eye twitched ever so slightly yet enough for her to notice.

"It's what every new chef would give up his favorite knife set for. Turns out your tenacity to move forward with this massive project will be quite a coup for us. It's exactly what we need to put Pennington Point Inn back on the map. The guests will love it. Of course, a lot is riding on the success of the clambake, including the inn's longstanding reputation, but you seem quite confident you can pull it off."

With that, she turned on her heel and pushed her way out of the kitchen, jamming the extra flyers into the can by the door, leaving her chef to contemplate what he'd gotten himself into. She hoped he regretted challenging her authority. Or was he patting himself on the back and feeling triumphant? Either way, she prayed she hadn't let him have his way for the wrong reasons.

CHAPTER ELEVEN

It *went against everything* she thought to be right. Everything the inn and the Pennington family stood for—over the years, now, and always. But Elizabeth was caught in a bind. Now that the newly renovated inn was finally open and sixty percent occupied—surprisingly successful in spite of a limited budget to advertise—the only downside was they didn't have adequate staff to handle the demands of the guests. Most were new and weren't familiar with the inn's procedures and protocol. And Elizabeth was spending too much time behind the desk, answering the phone, taking reservations, and coordinating rooms with housekeeping. Rashelle could slide right into her old position and hit the ground running, freeing up Elizabeth to manage at a more macro level. But no matter how much she tried to rationalize it was a good problem to have that somehow justified what she was about to do, the truth of the matter was Elizabeth was desperate and needed a qualified professional to slip into the role and handle the front desk operations, one that had experience—at Pennington Point Inn.

She'd hated making the call, crawling back after finally having the guts to stand up to Rashelle, asking her to stop by for a chat. Now she was practically begging her to return to the inn. But there had to be an understanding. Circumstances had changed. Shelle had changed them. This time there would be a probationary period during which she would be observed and critiqued. And Elizabeth could let her go at any time during that period. Her former friend from NYU said she understood.

"I'm serious, Shelle. I've given you too many chances as it is. This is your last."

"So why are you doing it?"

Was she really pushing back—giving Elizabeth reason to question her decision? "Shelle, why do you do *this*? Here I am offering you a job when you don't have any other options, and you're going to stand there and question my—"

"Oh, I've got other options. Don't kid yourself."

Yeah, bumming for spare change downtown during the day while evading arrest and crashing at the nearest homeless shelter at night—or worse.

"Why can't you appreciate that someone is extending their hand to you? And that you have something to offer them in return. This could be a win-win . . . unless you blow it." It took everything she had not to add "again" at the end, but the word manifested itself between them, even if it was unspoken. "So one more stipulation to our agreement that will help ensure your success is that you will attend AA meetings."

"*Hell*, no."

"Yes, that *is* what's going to happen." Elizabeth told herself this was in the best interest of the inn, not because she was acting as a friend.

"Aw, Lizzi, you can't be serious." Her shoulders slumped, and she dropped into the desk chair.

"I most certainly am serious. Don't think for a second that I'm not. Your drinking has been the root of your problems all these years, and if you can spare a shred of honesty for yourself, you'll admit it. I should have said something long before now." *Was Elizabeth admitting to being a terrible friend? How did it get twisted around so she was at fault?* "There is a local group that meets at the Congregational church in town. Every Monday evening at seven o'clock."

"Oh my gawd. You *are* serious."

"Of course, I am. And if you can't abide by that requirement, then I guess we don't have an agreement, and you don't have a job."

"And you don't have a front desk manager."

Elizabeth could feel the power shifting to Rashelle's side of the small space. She was manipulating the situation to suit her, as she'd done many times in the past. Rashelle knew Elizabeth had a gaping hole to fill, a key role at the newly opened inn, and she was the perfect fit. No training necessary. The success of the inn under Elizabeth's reign hinged on qualified, experienced staff that could ensure guests have an enjoyable visit, spread the word, and come back. Rashelle should be in that key role—and they both knew it. Elizabeth also knew Shelle was desperate, but she wasn't about to let on. She'd perfected hiding the truth.

"No I don't, but I'm not going to hire you into that position or any other position here unless you agree to all the stipulations."

"Lizzi, you can't do—"

"Oh, yes I can." Elizabeth muscled back her authority. "Look, Shelle, you are a talented woman. You have a lot to offer when you walk into a job in this industry. On paper, any employer would love to take you on. It's everything you wouldn't dare put on your résumé—everything you'd never bring up in an interview—that would do you in. Your attitude isn't always where it should be. Honesty takes a back seat when it's inconvenient. But both of those vices are the direct result of your drinking. And that has to stop. You owe it to me to make that happen, and more importantly, you owe it to yourself."

Rashelle fiddled with a thin metal bracelet at her wrist, spinning it round and round. Elizabeth remained silent, allowing her to consider everything she'd laid out for her, crossing her fingers they had an accord.

After depleting her lungs in a prolonged groan, Shelle clasped her hands together, rolling them from side to side. "All right. I'll help you out since you're in such dire need."

Once again, Rashelle had twisted the situation, making it sound like she was the one who was going out of her way to lend a hand. Elizabeth prayed she wouldn't be sorry for hiring her back. If only Shelle would uphold her end of the bargain, it could work. And they both would benefit. Realistically, the chance of that happening was highly unlikely. Hopefully, Elizabeth had at least bought herself some time.

In an effort to underscore her chef's rookie status while posturing Rashelle as a veteran, Elizabeth asked Vincenzo to come out to the front desk for introductions, away from "his" kitchen.

"Ah, Vincenzo. There you are. I'd like you to meet our day manager, Rashelle. Rashelle, this is our chef, Vincenzo." She purposely left off the word "head" or anything else that sounded authoritative.

As they shook, Elizabeth continued, "Rashelle is actually returning to this position. She was one of our seasoned staff at the original inn." Elizabeth reflected on the hurricane that almost blew it into oblivion after all the sordid events that nearly destroyed the inn's reputation. "We were fortunate to be able to entice her to return. She knows this place inside and out. Front and back. She might know it better than I do." She laughed and gave Shelle a playful tap on the shoulder. "She'll hit the ground running and pick up where she left off. No training period necessary. No learning curve. So if I'm not around and you have a question, feel free to ask her." Sensing she was venturing close to overdoing her endorsement, Elizabeth stopped there, trusting Rashelle understood her gesture, too.

CHAPTER TWELVE

"*W*hat do you mean*, you have to head back to Connecticut?" Kurt sat forward in his chair, setting his wine glass on the coffee table. The last sip of Cabernet sloshed against the sides. "You just reopened the inn."

"I know, but I've got clients I need to see. It will just be for an overnight."

"What are you talking about? I thought you closed your design business." Suddenly the fire needed stoking. He rose and grabbed the poker from the stand, stabbing the logs and releasing sparks that burst like fireworks.

"Well, I did get out of my lease for my office space, but I still have my condo, so I've been running my business out of the spare bedroom. I meet clients at their homes or places of business, so I don't really need office space." She retreated into her wingback, pulling her legs under her, regretting not being completely forthcoming with him. Had she been realistic thinking she could run her interior design business on the side—and keep it from him?

"Elizabeth, you've *got* to be kidding." He tossed the fire iron onto the stand with a clunk, leaving it askew. Sliding across the handles of the other tools, the poker pirouetted before hitting a corner stone at the fireplace base with a clank. He left it where it lay.

Buddy twitched and sat up at her feet.

"I had no idea. All this time you must have been spreading yourself thin trying to oversee the renovations here and continuing to run your business three states away."

"I've been able to manage." She wasn't going to acknowledge the distance between the two projects had proven so challenging she'd come close to throwing in the towel on both. "Besides, once the inn is profitable, I'm going to be hiring an assistant who will turn out to be a huge help, a quick study, I'm sure," she offered, sounding too exuberant to her own ears. But maybe she really didn't want someone so involved.

"Why are you insisting on designing?"

"Insisting?"

"All I'm saying is this place, alone, has got to be more than a full-time job. How can you do both well? . . . And apparently it's *not* going so well, given those damn property tax bills I discovered."

She ignored his last dig. "I love to design, Kurt. It's what I've always been meant to do." Who was he to question how she ran things? "I finally got out from under that tyrant Vera, left New York City behind, and forged out on my own. It's been my dream. I worked so hard to get the business started, and it was just starting to hum when—"

"Your conscience kicked in, and you realized you were supposed to take care of this place?" He took hold of the top of the wingback across from hers like he was anticipating a backlash.

She allowed her silence to settle between them. "That's not fair."

"I'm sorry, Elizabeth. I don't appreciate you not being totally up-front with me. When I said I would be happy to get involved and help you with running the inn, I expected it to be fifty/fifty. Not fifty/fifty except when you're out of town on a regular basis."

"I'm sorry. I wasn't sure how much of the time I would have to be away. I shouldn't have assumed you would cover for me."

"You're *damn* right. If this is going to work, it's got to be a partnership. And there has to be communication. You're setting us up for failure by making assumptions that involve me." He spun on his heels and headed toward the foyer. Steps from the hardwood floor he halted. "I'm going to have to give this some thought. I may have to reconsider my end of the commitment."

Eager to shake off the sting of his words, she set about righting the fireplace tools, retrieving the poker and returning it to its proper place in the stand. The mortar around the stone it had glanced off of appeared crumbled in places. Grabbing ahold of the cold smooth edges, she felt it shift slightly. *Great. Another repair for the growing list she already couldn't afford to take care of.*

As his footsteps faded away, Elizabeth threw down the last couple swigs and refilled her glass, jamming the empty bottle back into the bucket. Her grandmother would have said she was burning the candle at both ends, and you could only do that for so long before you had to pay the price. What was her price going to be?

Not expecting their conversation to spiral out of control as it had, she'd lost an opportunity to talk to him about the letter. She would need to find a less emotionally charged moment. Perhaps she didn't want to know. She felt him slipping from her grasp as it was.

CHAPTER THIRTEEN

"*Thought you'd be* long gone by now." Elizabeth slipped into the room they shared, pleased to see Kurt lingering longer than usual over his morning coffee by the window.

His grin had already pushed a dimple into his cheek when he turned toward the sound of her voice. "Not yet."

Not expecting to find him in such good spirits, Elizabeth felt relieved he seemed to let go of differences or an exchange of harsh words—and not just between the two of them—more quickly than anyone else she knew. "Listen, I'm sorry. I guess I'm so used to doing things on my own, only having me to worry about all these years. I wasn't considering how my decisions affected you . . . or anyone else for that matter." She recalled the scolding she'd gotten from Sam's father the first time she showed up at the inn after the hurricane. Reluctant to return to the place where she'd suffered such painful personal loss, she'd put off her visit for months. By the time she gathered the courage to go, the damage had been further exacerbated by the elements and neglect.

"Well, I gave that some thought. I also realized I'd been doing the same thing. Couldn't very well fault you. And I should have known you would try to do it all."

"But as you rightly pointed out, I really can't do it all—well."

He maintained his silence, reserving comment. She was grateful for his considerate restraint. It was hard enough hearing it the first time.

"The only problem is, I've made commitments that I need to honor."

His face showed the faintest of a flinch.

"And unfortunately, they're in Connecticut."

His arms slid onto his chest, folding firmly onto each other as he pushed back in the chair. "I'm sure you'll get it all figured out."

She hated when he said that or anything to that effect. And he seemed to have been saying it more frequently lately.

"But seriously, I thought you would have taken off, leaving me to fend for myself. Not that I could honestly blame you if you did."

"I can't say I didn't think about it. . . . But I told you I would join you in this venture, and I meant it."

A tickle fluttered through her abdomen. Elizabeth admired his integrity. It seemed so few men could be depended on for that—actually, either gender. Elizabeth had felt like an island throughout her adult life with few real connections with others. That was, until Kurt reappeared. She could only hope the bridge they'd formed between them turned out to be made of a sturdy reinforced steel that could weather any storm.

"I can't tell you how much I appreciate that, Kurt. It means the world to me." She brushed dark chestnut hair off his forehead and planted a kiss on his warm lips, holding back the urge to comment on the length of his hair. He slipped a strong arm around her waist and pulled her in. She didn't resist. He moved in and found her lips again, penetrating deeply. Releasing the tension in her shoulders, she allowed him to take control. Unfamiliar territory for her, but she was starting to get used to it. She liked being there and felt safe in his arms, like this was what she had been missing up until now.

Unwilling to spoil the moment, she put off asking him about the letter. It would have to wait awhile longer. Then again, she wasn't sure she wanted to have her questions answered. The status quo felt good.

CHAPTER FOURTEEN

Putting the inn in her rearview mirror, Elizabeth hit the road to Connecticut, dreading the long ride. She no longer had her sporty BMW z4 to tootle around in, having traded it in for a more practical Jeep Cherokee so her dear pup would have more space to stretch out when he rode with her. Leaving later than planned, the sun had long since set. Shadows of the pine trees carved by the moonlight hung across the road.

She had arranged to meet with three of her clients and hoped there were no further snags to keep her from wrapping up their projects. They'd dragged on long enough. And since customer satisfaction was the backbone of her business, it pained her that her clients were none too pleased with the delays. To add to the stress, she couldn't send a bill until a job was completed; but she needed the money.

As she passed the fork in the access road that veered off toward the lighthouse, her cell vibrated on the passenger seat. Though only intending to see if it was a text or a call, she snatched it up to take a quick peek. One of her clients. Was she canceling their appointment—again? Elizabeth didn't have time to make another trip back down to accommodate a single client. She was pushing her luck as it was. Kurt would be furious with her. The only saving grace was she'd left Buddy to keep him company.

Using the thumb of the hand holding the phone, she clumsily scrolled through the text, glancing from the screen to the road and back again. She focused a tad too long on the note explaining why the woman couldn't meet with her. Suddenly her cell flew out of her hand.

CHAPTER FIFTEEN

K*urt resented being left* to handle all the excruciatingly minute details of the day-to-day
operations. It wasn't his forte. He didn't give a *damn* if a Platinum
American Express Card-carrying guest wasn't happy he didn't
get the same ocean view he'd had three summers before. Or that
the vintage of the Cabernet Sauvignon delivered by room service
wasn't up to Manhattan standards. Sorry for the wake-up call, but
they were no longer in the big city.

With the inn in her blood, Elizabeth was better at keeping a
straight face and dealing with unreasonable demands. He admired
her innate ability. She made it look easy. He didn't think he could
ever get good at it and had no intention of trying. More than the
rest, he particularly resented having to deal with irritable Mrs.
Leibowitz. Her reputation was not unrealistic by any stretch. She
seemed to go out of her way to be insufferable.

If he was seriously considering asking Elizabeth for her hand, he needed to think long and hard if he could endure the drudgery on an ongoing basis—forever. He was more accustomed to being a free spirit. Not having to commit or become attached to any one place . . . or person. It had been convenient to devote himself to his job. Country first and foremost. No time for anyone else. Nothing serious, anyway. Could he really be happy reporting for work every day for the rest of his life at a quaint New England inn where the most exciting events were a round-robin tennis tournament and the monthly clambake on the beach? It was certainly a change in lifestyle, and he needed to consider if it was right for him.

Fortunately, Elizabeth was due back that evening, so he could hand over the reins. It couldn't happen soon enough. He wasn't cut out for smiling sweetly and nodding to keep customers happy. There were no customers at the FBI. Just slippery, evil thugs who spent their time eluding authorities and thinking up devious crimes with absolute certainty—fueled by their pathetically smug attitudes—they'd never get caught. Criminals in general were not the genius type, but it seemed the ones the FBI were after had a little more going for them. Initially they were able to get away, in some cases literally, with murder. But most couldn't keep the game going long enough to make a career out of it. The befuddled look on their faces once they were apprehended amused him. Some of them seemed sincerely shocked when their gig was up.

As the hour ticked closer to midnight, he glanced at his watch more frequently. Elizabeth hadn't been in touch since she'd left the previous day, but he knew she had an unrealistic schedule of meetings with clients and suppliers that filled every waking hour and then some. She'd probably worked until she dropped and only caught a few hours' sleep before jumping back in and picking up where she'd left off. He had hoped she would text to alert him she was setting out from Connecticut. When that didn't happen he sent her a message, but she didn't respond. He figured that meant she was focused on the road and not that she was annoyed with him.

Had he been too hard on her about this whole annoying interior design business? He feared her insistence on keeping it going would have a detrimental impact on the inn—one that couldn't be recovered from. He wished she could step back and see what she was doing and how it affected others.

Maybe this was her means of stepping away from the inn occasionally—to keep her sanity. Or was she taking a break from him?

He had passed the time with meaningless tasks, among them building a fire in the drawing room and keeping it stoked throughout the evening. Buddy seemed uneasy and kept close to Kurt's side. He tried to nurse his glass of Merlot, determined not to finish the second bottle but losing willpower as the evening progressed. The occasional guest would ring the front desk, asking for extra towels or looking for assistance with dinner reservations for the next day—to what purpose on the latter, he wasn't clear. They could just as easily pick up the phone and call the restaurant. It wasn't like he could work his magic and get them something above and beyond the norm. Maybe Elizabeth could. And when Hunter's manager had called to ask if he could arrange for a late-night pizza delivery, Kurt simply gave him the phone number for the local pizza chain that delivered.

By 1:00 a.m., he grew concerned. Calls and texts went unanswered. It was as if she'd simply vanished. Was he overreacting? Had he angered her to the point of not speaking to him? Was the wine making him paranoid? If he did call the police, which department would he try first? Her travels took her through three states into central Connecticut. Technically she hadn't been missing forty-eight hours yet. No one was going to take him seriously, but he didn't know how much more of the waiting he could endure.

His thoughts returned to his role as innkeeper. It galled him to think she expected him to fill her shoes in her absence. He'd had enough. He wanted out. Then again, if the current financial downward spiral continued, there wouldn't be an inn to worry about. He could go back to the Bureau and get his old job back. They'd be thrilled to have him. Already trained. With experience. And there would always be shit-eating bad guys to apprehend. Certainly a worthwhile line of work. And respectable. Actually making a difference in the world. Without having to kowtow to annoying guests or deal with a self-indulgent, belligerent chef. He certainly wouldn't miss any of that nonsense if he walked away.

Without a measure of guilt he emptied the remainder of the bottle into his glass as the glow of dying embers faded to black.

CHAPTER SIXTEEN

The sound of shattering glass woke him. Kurt jolted to the edge of the chair, his shoes crunching on what had been his wine glass. An uneasy stillness pervaded the dark drawing room. Coals in the fireplace had long since gone out. Dim light from a floor lamp in the corner glimmered off the shards scattered near his feet. Stirred by the sudden noise, Buddy nudged Kurt's hand, a safe distance from the broken glass on the opposite side of his legs. Three a.m. and Elizabeth hadn't come back yet. Surely she would have awakened him if she had.

Pushing past a dull Merlot headache, his thoughts returned to her possible whereabouts and her safety. Something had happened. She was in danger. Somewhere. She was hurt or worse. But no law enforcement officer would get involved before the requisite time frame had passed—at least no one who was unfamiliar with the Penningtons. So he would start with someone who was.

Deputy Austin slipped through the front door with little fanfare, easing the screen door closed with a soft click. His hair looked like he'd forgotten to run a comb through it before getting out of bed and slapping on his peaked hat. He rubbed his hand across the lower third of his face, presumably to mask a persistent yawn.

"Sam, I appreciate you coming. I know it's late."

The deputy remained silent but drew his mouth to the side with a slight tilt of his head, clearly perturbed to be summoned in the middle of the night.

"This isn't like her to not be in contact. I know she's really busy, but . . . I just have an awful feeling about this—especially with you having to investigate that other woman's death."

Sam perked up a bit, as if he hadn't made the connection before then.

Kurt shuddered. *C'mon, deputy. I need your help here. Get up to speed already. I shouldn't be three steps ahead of you. Help me find Elizabeth.* He couldn't bear the thought she might not make it back. God, he wished he hadn't been so hard on her. Had he really considered her side of things—how hard she was working to make it all happen? There were so many hurtful words he wished he could take back.

Together, they went through the standard list of questions. When she had left. What her plans were to return. When the last time was he'd heard from her. In the process, the deputy came up with an angle Kurt hadn't considered. Had he checked with friends?

The only one that came to mind was Rashelle. Were they really friends? Didn't matter. They had a connection, even if it was only through work. Potentially, she knew more about Elizabeth's whereabouts than anyone else.

It took several tries to rouse Rashelle by phone, and it was a few minutes before she made her way down the stairs to the lobby. In spite of the delay, she looked as though she hadn't bothered to freshen up. Her hair was pulled back into a pony, and she had an uncharacteristic lack of face paint. It struck Kurt there was something quite attractive in her eyes, usually hidden underneath layers of black makeup. She took a defensive stance, leaning against the registration counter with arms folded against her untucked green plaid flannel shirt.

"What's up?" Her voice was low and raspy. Her glare traveled between the two men, landing on Kurt as he spoke.

"Rashelle, I'm afraid something—" Concern caught in his throat. "—may have happened to Elizabeth." He was disappointed her expression remained fixed, not a twitch of acknowledgment. "She should have been back hours ago, and I can't reach her by phone."

Scowling, she snapped, "So why did you wake *me* up at—"

"Because we hoped you could help," Kurt retorted. He leaned in, pushing her back on her heels.

"How the *hell* would I know where she is? She doesn't report to me. I report to her."

"But you two are friends—at least you used to be."

"We're not friends." She glared. "And according to her, we never were." She turned and retreated toward the stairs.

"Well, you do work closely together," Sam piped up, stopping her in her tracks. "Have you been in contact with her recently? Did she share with you any plans that would have kept her away longer than expected?"

"No. I don't know anything more than you guys. If anything, I know a lot less. Now, I'm going back to bed. Don't wake me up again. You figure it out. You're trained law enforcement. Not me." She stabbed at the air with an accusatory finger.

With each fading footfall, Kurt's frustration grew. They had nothing to work with. No direction to head in.

The deputy pulled out his cell. "Let me make some calls . . . see what I can find out."

Kurt headed for his truck with Buddy at his heels. Even if he didn't know where to go, it was better than sitting still.

After what seemed like hours of driving around with no purpose other than to stay in motion, Kurt's cell sounded in the console. Pulling to the side, he snatched it up.

"Yeah." At that hour, it was either Elizabeth or Sam. Hoping for the former, he got the latter.

"Hey, Kurt. It's me."

"Where the hell have you been?"

"Been a little tied up on this end."

"Have anything?"

"Matter of fact, I do. Got ahold of the cell phone company to have them take a look at the towers to see if any of them got a ping from her phone."

"Geez, that could be anywhere between here and halfway into Connecticut. That will take a while."

"Well, I figured it was worth a shot. Must be a slow night for them. They already got back to me and said there was a ping on the tower near the inn yesterday evening but nothing after that."

"Nothing after that? So . . . she didn't use her phone after she left the inn? Turned it off?"

"Could be."

"I find that hard to believe. She's always on her phone in the car. Makes use of her time so she's always productive. Calling clients or suppliers . . . or someone on the staff here at the inn . . . me." His last thought hit him hard. Usually she called when they were apart, but she hadn't taken the time to text him while she'd been gone. Not like her. "Even if she didn't actively use her phone, as long as it was on, cell towers would receive a ping as she entered their range. Our phones are constantly using data to get e-mails and texts. And she always leaves her web browser open on her phone."

"Do you know who she had appointments with—who she was going to meet?"

"No. That was her business. She didn't feel the need to share any of that with me—not that I expected her to. . . . Maybe she didn't make any calls after the initial ping because she couldn't. Something happened to her—or her phone." Did she shut it off in retaliation for their heated discussion over her design business—to sever any possibility of him connecting with her? "Somewhere near the inn—"

"Exactly. It doesn't narrow down the search area. It just gives us a general area to work with."

"That's not a reason to stand here with our hands jammed down our pockets. We at least know where to start." Kurt shook his head, acknowledging how ridiculous he sounded. They were no further ahead than before Sam called. Useless information. He figured the deputy needed to look like he was working on the situation, pursuing all angles. "All right. Keep in touch." Tossing his cell back into the console, he turned the truck around and headed back to the inn.

As he turned onto the access road, he flashed back to the time he'd found Elizabeth along the side after tumbling down the embankment, having succumbed to severe fatigue, stress, and the summer heat. His gut was pulling him to return to the same location.

Throwing the truck into park, he switched on the high beams and fished the heavy-duty flashlight out from under the seat before climbing out of the cab. Time to scour the ditch.

Buddy let out a woof. "No, you stay there, Bud. I don't need you wandering off."

Setting off on foot, he walked along the edge, carving a zigzag swath into the darkness. He soon realized it would take a while to cover the entire access road working alone. Was he wasting his time? Should he be looking elsewhere? He had to start somewhere. Might as well be at the beginning.

Headlights approached from the main road and slowed to pass his truck. Its high beams backlit the outline of the light rack on the deputy's cruiser as Sam pulled up and leaned out the window.

"Whatcha up to, Mitchell?"

The first words that came to him were loaded with more sass than the deputy deserved at the early hour, so he rephrased his response, doing his best to harness his frustration. "I thought it was worth checking the ditches. A car could easily go off the side here. And in some places, it's fairly deep. It's possible a car could be out of sight from up on the road."

Sam seemed to be considering if the effort was worth the more-than-likely outcome—wasted time.

"You look where you want to. I'm starting here." Kurt resumed his search on foot.

"All right, let me ask you this: Would Elizabeth have stayed on the highways on her way to Connecticut and back again? She doesn't tend to take back roads or the scenic route, does she?"

"Oh, I think she would have stuck to the highways. Minimize her travel time. Why?"

"I called the state police in New Hampshire, Mass, and Connecticut to check on any reported accidents there. None involved a car that matched hers."

There was some comfort Kurt could extract from the deputy's update. But again, they were no further ahead.

"You sure you haven't heard from her because she's pissed off at you for some reason?"

"Nice, Sam. No, I don't think she's pissed off at me." As embarrassed as he would be if that were the case, he wished that was all this was about.

Apparently running out of his own ideas, Sam offered to help with Kurt's search.

"That would be helpful. Thanks. Why don't I grab my truck, and one of us can stand on the running board with the flashlight. See better up higher."

"I'll take the running board." The deputy staked out his claim and pulled the cruiser off to the side, switching on the rack lights.

Climbing onto the passenger side of the truck, he took the light from Kurt and grabbed ahold of the inside of the doorframe. Buddy's back end wagged as he sniffed at the deputy's hand and then settled back onto the seat, sitting upright. The three started down the dark road, snaking through the woods, leaving the flashing lights farther behind as they went. After the first curve, the cruiser was no longer in the rearview mirror.

The woods were eerily quiet. The sound of the engine seemed unusually loud as the truck crept along, tires crunching on loose gravel. Periodically, Kurt checked Sam's expression in the dim light, willing him to say something, see something. The first mile was behind them with nothing spotted.

While Kurt's focus was on the deputy, he caught movement in his peripheral and slammed on the brakes. Sam lost his grip and sailed off the running board and landed somewhere out of view with a grunt. Buddy scrambled to stay on the seat.

Kurt jammed it into park and jumped out of the cab. Just as he got around the front, Sam was clambering up the embankment.

"What the hell, Mitchell."

"I'm sorry. Raccoon ran across the road. Didn't see it 'til I was on top of it."

"Jesus. You damn near killed me. Pay attention," he scolded, brushing off his uniform, looking more embarrassed than angry.

Back on the truck again, they pressed along, searching for any sign of Elizabeth or her car. Soon they reached the fork, and Kurt bore to the left toward the inn, retracing her route. It wasn't long before they could see lights filtering through the trees.

As they circled around the drive in front of the inn, the only lights burning were those in the common areas. The guests seemed to be all tucked in and oblivious to Kurt's heartache and the agonizing reality that something may have happened to sweet Elizabeth.

Heading back down the road, he kept the truck at a steady speed, keeping an eye out for critters who might throw themselves in front of his tires and impede their progress. Not far along, Sam called out, "Whoa." Kurt stumbled out of the cab in his haste to see what had caught the deputy's attention. "Nah, it's nothing. Just some empty beer cans. The light flashed off them, and I thought it might be a bumper."

Deflated, Kurt jumped back up behind the wheel, and they kept going. He wondered if he should be glad they weren't finding anything. Did he really want to find Lizzi's car smashed up at the bottom of the embankment with her in it? He would be happy if she was just really mad at him.

Past the fork, they rounded the curve, creeping along toward the cruiser's flashing lights. Finally Sam yelled out. "Stop! There. Sticking out from under . . ." He'd hopped off and disappeared down the embankment.

Kurt couldn't get out of the truck fast enough, slamming the door behind him. He circled the front end and followed the deputy. Buddy let out a yelp. "Stay," Kurt yelled to the pup.

When he got close, he could see part of a bumper sticking out from under branches of a tree that had fallen, nearly covering the entire Jeep. When he saw the license plate, his heart sank. *Dear God, please don't take her from me.*

Shining the light across the back end, the deputy lifted the ends of branches revealing broken brake lights and a dented bumper. Did the damage occur on the way down the embankment—or from someone hitting her from behind?

At the moment, determining how she got there wasn't paramount. Kurt needed to get to her and get her out. Diving for the driver's side, he grabbed the branches to pull them free, but they wouldn't let go.

"Sam, get in here and give me a hand."

The two got some leverage and slid the tree trunk enough to clear the door, which was heavily damaged. While Sam shone the light inside, Kurt lunged at the handle. It wouldn't budge. He yanked and yanked, but it wouldn't give.

He could see the airbag had deployed. Snatching the light away from the deputy, he put it up to the window.

"Elizabeth!" The top half of her body was splayed across the middle console. Her seat belt still fastened. "Dear God, please let her be okay," he whispered.

"I'll be right back." Sam disappeared up the bank while Kurt tried to rouse Elizabeth.

"Lizzi, wake up. It's me. Kurt." He pounded on the top of the car in exasperation. "Liz, c'mon. Wake up. Can you hear me?" He kept pounding.

Sam returned with a baton he used as a battering ram, shattering the back window. Reaching inside he pulled the lever and opened the door, scooting onto the seat. Seconds later he emerged. "I got a pulse."

While the deputy called for an ambulance and backup, Kurt slipped in, brushing shards of glass from the seat with his palm. "Liz." Her neck was warm to the touch. Thankfully it wasn't the middle of winter. Relieved, he brushed hair from her face, alarmed to see dried blood had dripped from a cut on her cheek. *Please be okay.* He touched her neck again to confirm the pulse. It was faint, but existent.

With the passenger side of the car wedged against the dirt embankment, the firemen used the Jaws of Life on the driver's door and then cut through the seat belt that was jammed. By the time they hauled her out and eased her onto the stretcher, she started to come to.

Kurt moved in and took her hand. "It's going to be all right, Lizzi. You're safe now." Dark black and blue circles under her eyes made her look like a rookie boxer who'd gone down in a title match. He was grateful to feel the warmth of her hand.

Squinting past a flashlight, she found his face among those bobbing around her, and she squeezed his hand. In a feeble voice she asked, "What took you so long?"

As the EMTs loaded her into the back of the ambulance, Kurt found Sam and grabbed him firmly by the upper arm. The deputy pulled back, looking indignant but unable to break free from his grasp.

"You find who did this to her. They undoubtedly know they didn't finish the job, and they'll be back." Kurt remained latched on to his arm.

"What makes you think this is anything other than distracted driving?"

"Didn't you see the damage to the rear bumper?" Kurt leaned in.

Sam pulled back. "That could have happened on the way into the ditch."

"I'll bet if you check out the car in daylight, you'll find paint that's transferred from another vehicle."

"Well, it could have been unintentional, and the person was afraid and took off for whatever reason."

"Either way, you need to find out what happened. She deserves that."

"I will. I'm on it." Sam tried again to pull from his grip, and this time Kurt let him go.

"Fast. We don't have a lot of time. . . . If this was intentional, you know they'll be back."

CHAPTER SEVENTEEN

After an overnight at the hospital, Elizabeth was cleared to be discharged. The consensus was the airbag had done more damage than getting hurled down the embankment. She was sent home with instructions on how to nurse a mild concussion.

Her head felt as though it was detached at the neck and floating over her shoulders. She tried to blink away the dizziness. It was hard to ignore the buzzing in her ears.

When Kurt walked through the door to drive her home, she burst into a grin and couldn't stop smiling. Her proverbial knight in shining armor with an adorable glint in his eye was there to carry her away. She grabbed on and didn't want to let go. Finally they pulled apart, but she hung on to his arm.

"I got your cell back from Sam." He held it out to her. "They finished processing your car."

"Yeah, the damn thing went flying. Had no idea where it was. Couldn't get out of my seat belt to look." She swallowed hard. "I was so scared no one would find me. Thought I'd still be there for the first snow."

He wrapped a strong arm around her waist. "I would never have given up."

She slid into his arms again and squeezed. He stroked her back with a warm palm.

"When I woke up I didn't know where I was." She spoke into his chest. "It looked like I had landed in a tree."

"Well, not exactly. The tree came to you. And you were well hidden, for sure. No one driving by would have seen you."

She hated to ask but needed to know the answer. "So what happened? Did I just drive off the edge of the road? Good God. I don't remember a thing."

Kurt's hesitation said there was more to the story. Did there always have to be?

"I'd have to say from the preliminary—"

"Just lay it out for me. Don't try to save me from the truth."

With his head cocked, he said, "All right. . . . You had a little help getting into the ditch."

"A little help?"

"Yeah. Your rear bumper was banged in pretty good. And unless you backed into a cement wall right before you left, I'd say—"

"Okay, I get it. Great." She could do her own introspective speculation. Who was nasty enough to hit her and not stick around to help?

"Sam has the state police keeping an eye out for a vehicle with a banged-in front bumper." He took her hands in his and pulled her close. "Thank goodness you weren't driving your old z4. A sports car like that wouldn't have fared as well hurtling into a ditch."

"Okay. Great. Let's get outta here." She'd had her fill of bad hospital food, a roommate who snored, and a terribly unflattering—not to mention revealing—johnny.

CHAPTER EIGHTEEN

"*So I have to ask.* You've been rather evasive about it in the past. But what was going on in your life between when I left you sitting in a bar in Manhattan and when I found you stalking me in front of my office building in Connecticut?"

Feeling more like herself with only a mild headache to remind her of her ordeal in the ditch, Elizabeth settled into the wing chair adjacent to the fireplace. Her pup curled up at her feet. Hoping he would cover the topic of a previous fiancée to save her from having to bring up the mysterious letter, she was curious where he would wind the conversation.

An amused smirk crept onto his face as if he was wrestling to keep it at bay. "Wondering if I've been up to no good?"

"And please don't say you can't tell me—that it's classified. You can talk in general terms."

His pretense of joviality faded away, but he gave no hint he had intentions of sharing.

"Look, I need to know. So much of what went on in your life is a complete secret. But I know some of it had to do with me or affects me—especially what delayed your decision to track me down."

He paused, considering her pointed request. "It actually had nothing to do with work, that is, the time that lapsed after I last saw you in New York City." He scooted to the edge of his chair.

That was unexpected. She'd had visions of him being sent to some far-flung Third World country where communications were limited, if not nonexistent. If it had nothing to do with his job, what was it? Did it involve the woman who claimed to have been engaged to him? Elizabeth remained silent and kept her body still, yearning for him to elaborate. Finally, he pulled back from wherever his thoughts had taken him.

"There was a—a situation—that came up with my family. My parents needed my help. My support." He wrung his hands as if there was something he needed to shed.

"Your parents?" This was the first she'd heard him mention them. Not having grown up with her own, she rarely pictured others having any.

"Yeah. At the time they lived up in Waterville, near the campus of Colby College. They were professors there. My dad taught history, my mom—art."

"That's where you went to college."

"Yeah, practically grew up on campus. But after I graduated, I took off and went to work with the FBI, so I didn't see them very often. I think it was hard on them, especially my mom. When I did show up—mostly for major holidays—I couldn't talk about what I was doing."

"So what happened?" Elizabeth's eyes met his, which were uncharacteristically cold and dark. "I'm sorry. I don't mean to push." He raised a palm to her and continued.

"My younger brother—much younger, fourteen years—arrived at a time that I found inconvenient. Who knows, maybe he wasn't planned. I don't know. Never asked that question. My parents were busy with their teaching and research careers and expected me to shoulder some of the babysitting responsibility. Quite a bit of it, it felt like. As far as I was concerned, he couldn't have shown up at a worse time. I was in high school, starting to taste my own freedom. He wasn't a bad kid or anything. It was just that, at the time, all I wanted was to do things with my friends. But my parents made it clear my priority was him. So I did the best I could to watch out for him, figuring I was biding my time before I could take off and have my college experience someplace new and far away from Waterville, Maine."

"Where did you want to go?"

He snorted. "Oh, it doesn't really matter now. That was ancient history. Old dreams and aspirations. The point is, they squashed them and let me know I'd be attending Colby. They really couldn't afford anywhere else—I don't know why I thought it was even a possibility—and I could get a free ride there. Guess I was too much of a dreamer."

"I'm sorry." It was all she could come up with.

"Yeah, well, you might as well hear the rest of it."

"You don't have to continue if you don't—"

"If we're going to get to know each other—I mean, really well—you've got to hear the good, the bad, and the ugly. And this ugly got worse. . . . Senior year of college, one afternoon he was just being a kid—"

"What's his name?" She nearly jolted from his sharp glance.

"Jamie . . . James, but we all called him Jamie. Except for my mom."

Elizabeth caught her breath. He'd used past tense.

"He had a skateboard accident. He was only seven. Hit a tree and suffered a traumatic brain injury." With pain etched across his face, he followed the lines in the floorboards to the dark ash-stained fireplace.

She could only whisper, "I'm so sorry."

Kurt sat motionless, reflections of the fire flickering on his face. Finally he broke the silence. "He was paralyzed from the neck down. The doctors gave him no chance of walking again." He found Elizabeth's empathetic eyes. "I think it almost killed my mother. My father's way of dealing with it was to shut down and not talk about it. My mother spent the next few years trying to make life as comfortable for Jamie as she could. She gave up teaching and devoted her days to caring for him. After graduation I escaped the constant reminder of his misery by accepting the job with the FBI and taking assignments wherever they wanted to send me. The farther away, the better. When I got sent to Pennington Point two and a half years ago, part of me panicked 'cause I was suddenly closer to home than I'd been in years. I knew I'd have to reconnect with them, but I put it off, using my work schedule as an excuse."

"Did you go see them eventually?" She spoke softly, endeavoring to convey her compassion.

"Not right away. In fact, I didn't make the first move. It was my father who tracked me down not long after you and I parted ways in New York that day. He called to tell me Jamie was very sick, and they didn't know if he was going to make it. At that point he was bedridden and had gotten pneumonia." He threw his head back as if trying to shake off the pain. "I knew what I had to do, so I took a leave of absence from the Bureau and headed north. I stayed with them and helped care for Jamie. It was excruciating to see him like that." Kurt rubbed his forehead. "He seemed to get better right after I got there, and my mother was so hopeful he would pull out of it. A couple months later he suddenly got worse and died. I've never cried so hard in my life."

Elizabeth moved over onto the edge of the loveseat next to his chair and slipped her arms around him. His upper body began to heave with sobs. Finally he gathered himself and pulled away from her slightly. She understood and slid back. Her pup moved over to be at her feet again.

"After the funeral, my parents cleared out of Waterville. Too many awful memories there. My father took an early retirement. He'd already cut his teaching hours, so he was more like a part-time adjunct professor. The college loved him, so they had let him teach as much as he was able. But at that point, my parents made the decision to move to Monhegan."

"Monhegan? Wow, that's quite a lifestyle change." Elizabeth regretted her choice of words. "What I mean is, island living is not for everyone. Although, I've always loved Monhegan. It's such a special place—but in the warmer months. I don't know that I could be there year-round, especially when the population drops to a few hearty souls after all the summer residents have cleared out. They'd have to be able to withstand the isolation and the bitter cold and rely on the supply boat's unpredictable schedule when the weather doesn't cooperate." She hated how her nerves made her ramble.

With the welcome sound of his chuckle, she was relieved to see his sense of humor returning. "Yeah, I've been in plenty of situations in my job where conditions were less than comfy, but I'm not sure I would willingly go through a Maine winter ten miles off the coast, out on a scrap of a rock with no guarantee of regular food deliveries."

She reached over and patted his abdomen. "Always about the food, isn't it?"

"*Absolutely.* A man's gotta eat."

They shared a laugh, and then he continued. "They didn't seem to have an issue with all of that, so I helped them make the move. I think they were looking for a solace you can only find on an island after the tourists have hopped back on their chartered boats. My mom wanted to get back to her painting, and my father had planned to write a book. An historical fiction of some sort."

Her body stiffened as she detected his use of past tense again. "What a great place to do both. How long have they been there?"

she ventured with a shred of optimism he wouldn't have to redirect her question.

"It's been a little over a year, so they've endured one winter so far, and I don't think it was nearly as bad as the island had had in previous years. But they used up a lot more wood in their stove than they'd planned on, so my dad amped up his cutting and splitting logs for this coming winter. Apparently he's got quite an impressive pile."

"That's good. I hope they're finding what they need there."

"Thank you. They seem to be . . . so far."

"It's such a beautiful island. I haven't been in years, but I have such fond memories."

Her thoughts went to the artists who lugged paint-filled tackle boxes with a canvas tucked under one arm and an easel under the other, staking out the best vantage points to paint from all over the island. Sometimes they would turn up in the most unexpected places.

Views from the lighthouse that went on forever were well worth the hike up the hill. A small history museum housed in it was a local treasure, and the rotating exhibits at the art museum nearby on the bluff drew art aficionados from far and wide. An extensive network of hiking trails crisscrossed the island, and a couple small beaches enticed beachcombers looking to take a dip in the frigid water or to set out on kayaks. A couple quaint shops catered to tourists, as did the aptly named Island Inn, the largest and most majestic of all the lodging options. Charming cottages of gray cedar shingles were tucked behind picket fences along the narrow dirt road, many of which boasted colorful gardens bursting with poppies, sunflowers, lilies, and if you were lucky to catch their short blooming period, lupines. With the exception of a couple pickup trucks used to carry deliveries from the dock, no vehicles were allowed. When the sun set after the last boat departed, a hush fell on the island that was innately peaceful, and the stars were brighter and more numerous than could be seen on the mainland. It was a small island—not five square miles—but it held a special place in her heart.

A corner of his mouth turned up, creating a dimple in his cheek. "I'd love to take you there. . . . I'd like you to meet my parents. They'd fall in love with you like I have."

She leaned over, wrapped her hands around his solid torso, and squeezed. His strong arms cradled her back.

"I'd love that."

She'd have to broach the topic of the letter with the engagement ring some other time.

CHAPTER NINETEEN

A couple raps on the office door to alert Rashelle to her arrival and Elizabeth slipped inside.

"How's it going?" she asked, keeping her tone upbeat.

With shoulders pulled back, Rashelle studied her before answering, lingering on the black circles under Elizabeth's eyes. "Just fine." Her tone dripped with resentment, clearly not moved by her boss' brush with death.

Elizabeth stood her ground. "Good to hear. Do you have any questions? Anything need my attention?"

Rashelle seemed to be straining not to react to Elizabeth's intrusion.

"No. . ." The single word was drawn out with deliberate undulation.

"I see. Well, could you give me a status on the current reservations?"

"A status. Like a percentage of capacity?"

"That would be great. What are we looking at right now?"

"I don't know off the—" She started with voice raised but caught herself and backed off. "I'd like to double-check the numbers before I give you an answer."

"Okay, let me know what you come up with. I'd like to stay on top of it. And if you can project out for the next couple of weeks, that would be great. Thanks."

As Elizabeth turned to head out, the contents of the trashcan next to Rashelle's chair caught her eye. A few pieces of discarded mail. She reached down and pulled out a familiar business-sized envelope addressed to her. The one with the cheap ring enclosed. By the feel of it, the ring was still inside.

"What's this?"

"What's what?" Rashelle echoed, throwing it back into Elizabeth's lap.

"This envelope, addressed to me. Handwritten, I might add." She shook the envelope at her. "What's this doing in the trash?"

"Oh, I guess it got scooped up with the junk mail. Sorry about that." She didn't seem any sorrier than if she'd carelessly squished a bug on the sidewalk.

"Shelle, this is a personal letter . . . addressed to me. How could you mistake it for junk mail?" And hadn't Elizabeth shoved it in the back of the top desk drawer so no one else would run across it inadvertently?

"It must have gotten stuck to something else. Like one of those half a dozen credit card offers you get on a daily basis with the open address window. Must have gotten caught in one of those."

"Rashelle, that's ridiculous. No such thing happened, and you and I both know it."

Grabbing her tangle of bracelets to fiddle with, the Brooklyn transplant clammed up. She was done defending herself. That was her explanation, and that was all there was to it.

Unable to prove otherwise, Elizabeth turned to take her leave, unsure why her day manager would have tossed out mail that was clearly personal. Desperate to exert her authority, she pressed, "Well, from now on, I'll go through all of the mail. Leave it all untouched for me to look at, even if you think it looks like junk." Certain she'd wedged another proverbial spike between them, Elizabeth couldn't help but notice Rashelle had grown more subdued since her return. Had Elizabeth treated her too harshly and completely broken her spirit? Of greater concern were Rashelle's motives to discard the letter. Had she read it? Or worse, had she written it?

The clanging of the desk phone brought them both back to their priorities—the guests. Rashelle answered and soon pulled the receiver away from her ear. Elizabeth could tell it was Mrs. Leibowitz on one of her rants. Rashelle could only shake her head and mutter "uh-huh" or "I see." Finally, she was able to jump in and assure their hysterical guest that they'd handle the situation. Hanging up, she turned to Elizabeth.

"Apparently, Eli and his crew are acting up in the room next to Mrs. L. She says they're having a wild party."

Elizabeth emptied her lungs and hung her head. This was exactly what she'd feared when she booked the group. "Great."

"They're just blowing off a little steam. Half the group was supposed to go out on a whale watch this afternoon, but the trip got canceled because of the rain, and the other half had a tee time that got washed out. Would you like me to take a walk over and tell them to settle down?"

"Really?"

"Are you kidding? I've been dying to meet him. I may be a city girl, but I'm a huge fan. I was hoping I'd bump in to him at some point, but it hasn't happened."

"All right, go for it. But try to let him down easy." She grinned, scrunching up her nose.

"Will do." Rashelle snatched the master key from the last slot under the counter to allow her to gain access to the building and headed out.

Elizabeth had the nagging feeling she was letting Rashelle walk right into the lion's den.

CHAPTER TWENTY

A teetering stack of mail had found its way into Elizabeth's inbox. Now that she'd established the protocol on how it would be handled, it was her responsibility—not that she needed to be taking on more, but that was how it ended up.

A corner of a cream-colored envelope stuck out from the rest of the mail, mundane in appearance and full of bills. Elizabeth pulled it out to read it first. There was no return address. No stamp. No postmark. Only Elizabeth's name written in gold ink in elegant cursive that resembled calligraphy. There was a gracefulness to it she hadn't seen since her grandmother was alive and left her a cherished note from time to time. The envelope had a thickness to it like an old-fashioned wedding invitation with the extra weight to match. Carefully sliding a finger under the flap, she tried to open it without tearing. Something special lay inside.

Shiny gold foil lined the flap and interior, surrounding a single ivory page of heavy card stock. Given the color, it could easily have been a keepsake from long ago. Elizabeth slid out an invitation in the same ornate handwriting—but not to a wedding.

The Pleasure of Your Company is Requested

Afternoon Tea

Next Wednesday, Three O'clock

The Pennington Point Inn

Pennington Point, Maine

A Friend

It was as intriguing as it was brief. But how did it get there? Was Kurt being creative in carving out time for the two of them to spend together? He certainly couldn't have produced that kind of handwriting. It had to be a female. Perhaps an older woman. But who?

Afternoon Tea was a recent addition to the calendar, one that Vincenzo had balked at, citing the need to prep for dinner instead. Yet Elizabeth remained firm and insisted he handle it. After all, if he was so certain he could pull off a clambake without a hitch, a tea should be a breeze. Her grandmother would have loved the idea.

She checked the reservations, and none had been made for the following Wednesday. Walk-ins would certainly be honored and, in all likelihood, it might take a while for the event to catch on. Elizabeth hoped to spread the word with a blurb she was able to get placed in the "What's Happening?" section of the local paper. One thing seemed certain: There would be at least two in attendance at the inaugural event.

When Wednesday finally arrived, Elizabeth was pleased with the turnout for the first Afternoon Tea. She had hired a couple of high school girls to help in case it was well attended and was relieved she'd incurred the moderate expense. By the time the grandfather clock in the foyer struck quarter past three, a steady stream of arrivals had filled most of the seats.

With the exception of a group of eight from a local book club, most of the other tables held two ladies; a few sported wide-brimmed, pastel-colored hats. One elderly woman sat alone along the windows as if waiting for a friend to join her. When their eyes met, Elizabeth realized she was the mystery friend who had sent the invitation.

As she neared, the woman lifted her head and managed a weak smile. Her folded hands— so delicate they looked like it would take only a gentle rap to shatter them—rested on the edge of the table. Her skin was like porcelain.

"You must be Elizabeth." Her voice was barely audible in the din of the room.

"Yes, I am."

"I knew I would recognize you even though it's been years. You have your father's eyes . . . and your mother's beautiful silky brown hair. So good to see you."

Elizabeth pulled out the chair across from her and slipped in, intrigued by the encounter.

"And I'm sorry, but I don't know that we've met."

The woman's smile returned momentarily before slipping away again. "It was a long time ago. You were quite small. So I'm sure you don't remember." She let out a guttural chuckle, startling Elizabeth for a moment. "Of course, I looked a little different back then."

Elizabeth examined her face, not able to recall seeing her at Amelia's funeral. She had a striking resemblance to her grandmother; snow-white and wavy hair framing her face, thin silver wire-rimmed glasses resting halfway down her nose, a faint sparkle behind them.

"Your grandmother and I were childhood friends. I grew up here in Pennington Point." Her voice warbled in a badge of honor that came with age. "I married my high school sweetheart who joined the navy, and he whisked me away from here . . . far away." Her heavy gaze drifted through the window and out to the horizon as if recalling her travels. "It wasn't an easy life. We moved a lot. And I never really came back. That is, until several months ago. My dear Andy passed away, and I came back to bury him here." She rubbed the end of her nose with a frail finger as she sniffled. "I was sorry to learn that dear Amelia passed a couple years ago. I should have known that was why her letters stopped."

"Yes, it was quite sudden . . . and absolutely heartbreaking." Lizzi swallowed hard to clear the lump forming in her throat.

The woman leaned in and looked like she wanted to reach out and touch Elizabeth but thought better of it. "I can imagine. I'm so sorry. Tea?" She abruptly changed the subject, gesturing toward a pink rose-covered teapot.

"Yes, that would be lovely. Allow me to pour." As Elizabeth lifted the porcelain pot, she couldn't imagine the old woman being able to manage the hefty weight of the full container. She would have to remember to direct the staff to be aware of guests' limitations like that.

Following up with the cream and sugar, to which her guest passed on, Elizabeth then offered the plate of cookies, which she declined as well. An orange pecan scone and a shortbread cookie found their way onto Elizabeth's plate.

"So you mentioned you and my grandmother were childhood friends. And you kept in contact over the years?"

"Oh, yes." Her tired eyes lit up. "We wrote to each other all the time. Kept up to date on what was going on in each other's lives. I missed her wedding because Andy was stationed in Hawaii. The trip back would have been . . . well, it just wasn't meant to be. We talked about getting together at some point, but Andy and I ended up on the West Coast, and the trip back East always seemed like something I would do eventually; but I didn't get back here until it was too late."

"So what made you get in contact with me now? Why the mysterious invitation?"

Her chuckle returned. "Oh, I thought that would be fun. I knew you wouldn't know who I was, and I thought if it came from me, you might turn down my invitation to meet, or worse— ignore it."

At first, Elizabeth grew indignant at the suggestion but then realized the old woman had a point. With everything going on at the inn, she may very well have put the invite from a stranger to the side or politely declined, using her workload as an excuse. But the intrigue of a secret caller—a mysterious rendezvous—was too tempting to pass up.

"I have something I think you should have."

Elizabeth returned her teacup to its saucer and waited for the woman to continue.

She nodded toward a small sheet of lined paper, the edge of which was tucked under her peach-colored napkin, still folded and held down by the silverware.

"What is it?" It appeared to have cursive writing on it.

"It's a page from a diary—Amelia's diary."

Elizabeth didn't recall her grandmother keeping one.

"I think you'll find if you insert this page in exactly the right spot, you'll have the complete instructions to find the treasure."

"What? What treasure?" Was the old woman recalling a child-hood game they'd played and never quite finished?

"Oh, you'll have to find out for yourself. It would take the fun out of it if I told you."

"But why don't you go after it?"

The woman bowed her head. "I'm afraid it would take a much more agile person than I. . . . And I have affairs to settle. Things to set straight. This is one of those things."

With that, the woman stood. "Good luck with it, Elizabeth. It was a pleasure to see you again." She slipped from the table and toddled across the dining room, abandoning a full cup of tea.

Elizabeth leaned across, curious to see what was written on the diary page. There were what appeared to be several lines in her grandmother's handwriting. *How exciting was the prospect of a treasure hunt?* Tickled, she never knew the woman who'd raised her had left behind something so clever.

Leaving the page where it lay, Elizabeth dashed to catch up to the old woman only to reach the door to the front porch and find no one in sight. Clearly not planning to stay long, she must have had someone waiting in the drive for her.

She'd never caught the woman's name.

Returning to the table they'd shared, she was horrified to see it had already been cleared. Bursting into the kitchen, the staff with the exception of the chef looked up.

"Who just cleared the small table along the windows? The two-person table. The one where I was sitting. It had a teapot with pink roses on it." She scanned the counters, looking for the familiar pot. When her query was met with shrugs and puzzled expressions, she dove into the nearest trashcan, picking through half-eaten cookies, soggy tea bags, and scrunched up napkins covered in coffee grounds. When she'd reached elbow deep, she pulled her arms out. "Where the *hell* is it?" A slimy film coated her arms as she repeated her search in the other two receptacles.

The rest of the kitchen resumed their duties, casting a wary glance in her direction from time to time.

Lunging at the sink, she washed up quickly and made a lap around the kitchen, eyes darting in a zigzag, before heading back out. Where could it be? Did someone take it? Without the mysterious guest's name, Elizabeth had no way to try to contact her. Even if she could, would the old woman be able to remember the details on the page?

Not wanting to disturb the pleasant hum of patrons chatting over tea, she conjured a pleasant smile and meandered through the tables, stopping to check on each one; scooping up half-empty cookie plates, replenishing them from a tray on a sideboard, and lifting the lids of teapots to see which ones needed refilling. No errant diary page in sight.

Then she spied it. The pink rose-covered pot. It was sitting on a stand, off to the side along the wall opposite the windows. Straining to keep from running, she made her way over in swift sliding steps. As she reached it, a voice came from behind.

"I'll get that, Ms. Pennington."

It was one of the high school girls, sidling up to grab the tray.

"Oh, Mackenzie. Thank you. Uh—" She put out a hand to stop her. "So did you clean off the small table along the windows?" She pointed in the general direction.

"Is something wrong?" The girl's eyes grew wide.

"No, no. There's not a problem. I'm just looking for something. That's all," the matron of the inn assured her.

Visibly relieved, the girl pulled her hands from the tray.

Elizabeth rummaged through the contents, lifting the pot and the plates to look underneath. "Where is it?"

"What are you looking for?"

"It's a sheet of paper. Lined. Like something out of a . . . small notebook."

"I see. Okay, well, I didn't see it, but I'll keep an eye out for it."

"Thank you. I appreciate that." What else could she ask? There was nothing left to do. Devastated she'd carelessly lost a precious link to her grandmother, Elizabeth admonished herself before returning her focus to more immediate matters. "And I want to thank you for helping out today. You're doing a great job. Everyone seems to be enjoying the tea. It's turned out better than I imagined."

"You're welcome, Ms. Pennington. Thank you for the opportunity."

Perplexed by the missing diary page and the mysterious visitor over tea, Elizabeth wondered if her grandmother had ever kept a diary. Although it wasn't something she'd ever mentioned, it certainly could be possible. But where would she have hidden it? The room she'd kept when she was alive had been cleared out to transform it into a guest room, and nothing resembling a diary was found. Although it tore at Elizabeth's heart to allow guests to stay where her grandmother once slept, she couldn't justify taking the expansive room for herself when she could charge more money for the extra space. She did, however, move the hope chest that once stood at the foot of Amelia's bed into her own room but had yet to go through it.

Suddenly, there was an urgency to discover exactly what the cedar chest held.

CHAPTER TWENTY-ONE

As long as *Elizabeth* could remember, the skeleton key had always rested in the lock under the lid of the chest. It was locked, but apparently no one had felt the need to remove the key and store it elsewhere, out of sight. At first, it resisted when she turned it. Pressing it in farther, she coaxed the key, and it turned with a dull click. The lid felt heavier than it looked, but the hinges held it in place above the chest filled to the brim. The aroma of cedar tickled her nose.

Although it gave the appearance it was merely stuffed with extra blankets, Elizabeth suspected there was more to be seen underneath. She scooped up neatly folded wool and cotton coverlets and lined them up on the bed like stepping-stones. Returning to the chest, she carefully lifted out an oversized, worn leather Bible, the corners of which were crumbling. She opened it to the inside cover and found a drawing of a family tree with many handwritten names and dates filled in. Locating her parents' names above her own, she was intrigued their birthdates were only four days apart, making a mental note to observe some sort of remembrance for them going forward.

Next to where the Bible lay was a lumpy, oblong shape wrapped in a small tattered pink and ivory quilt. Cradling it like a newborn, Elizabeth unwrapped the bundle to find a baby doll with a lifelike porcelain face that appeared fast asleep until she tilted it upright. It was dressed in a long lace-trimmed cotton gown with matching booties, resembling a christening outfit. Under the clothes, the stuffed muslin body was water-stained and appeared hand-stitched. Tiny hands and feet were also made of porcelain. Elizabeth could only guess the doll's age and origin, since anyone who would have had knowledge of the antique treasure had already passed away.

After rewrapping the doll closely resembling the way she'd found it, she dove in to tackle the rest of the chest. A thin, flat stationery box was filled with letters to her grandmother. From her grandfather? She couldn't resist poking into the one on top to confirm the sender. Torn by her curiosity to read the intimate messages and her instinct to respect Amelia's privacy, she secured the letters back inside the box.

Another contained notes and cards from Amelia's only grand-daughter, collected from when Elizabeth could first write in awkward, childlike scrawl to the last birthday card before her grandmother passed. It looked like she'd saved everything Elizabeth had ever written, including a note she'd left before heading off to the lighthouse for a painting session. Old grade school report cards kept company with class pictures. To keep from getting lost down memory lane, she returned the treasures and placed the container next to the first box on the bed.

With the hope chest nearly empty, the final layer consisted of a couple colorful wool Fair Isle sweaters, a fox stole that still held a slight mothball scent, and a cozy angora wrap. But no diary. She reasoned it may have been ruined during the hurricane when the inn suffered extensive damage, rendering it unrecognizable, and was tossed out. So she was back to where she started before she'd received the mysterious invite. No diary and no missing page that had been ripped out of it so long ago. In hindsight, it had been a long shot.

As she began to repack the chest in the reverse order the items came out, there came a knock at the door. It was the young girl who had cleared their table at tea.

"Ms. Pennington, is this what you were looking for?" She held out the diary page pinched between her thumb and forefinger.

"Yes, it is. Thank you. Where did you find it?" Elizabeth grasped it by the edges like it was a fragile, antique document, holding it out in front of her.

"It was under the table. I'm afraid it's been stepped on, though. I didn't notice it until someone, who sat at the table after you, caught it on the bottom of their shoe when they got up to leave."

"That's wonderful." Her eyes landed on familiar handwriting. "Thank you so much for finding it."

"No problem." The young girl slipped out, closing the door behind her.

But with no diary to insert the page into, she was still at a dead end. Elizabeth laid it on the bedside table and resumed her task of refilling the chest. As she scooped up the last coverlet from the bed, there was a soft thud on the floor next to her foot. The diary.

CHAPTER TWENTY-TWO

As a stand-alone document, the diary page bore little meaning. It was blank on the back side and on the front, "23" had been scribbled in the lower right corner. It wasn't until Elizabeth slipped it into place at the precise location of the ragged edge near the binding that directions started to make sense.

Inside the diary, the lower half of page twenty-two read:

> *To find the key that will lead you*
> *To the priceless treasure to own.*
> *Find the pattern that looks like steps*
> *Within a structure made of stone.*

It was just vague enough to leave a reader hanging without the detached page twenty-three which continued:

In the dead of a long, cold Maine winter,
You'll want to draw near the ingle roaring inside.
But don't look past the cracks in the mortar
Lest you miss the one you can wiggle and glide.

Elizabeth hadn't known her grandmother to be much of a poet. Perhaps her friend had lent a hand. But what had they meant with their enigmatic poem? One of the words threw her. Unfamiliar with the word "ingle," she grabbed her phone and looked it up.

A fire in a fireplace. So why call it an ingle? Why make it more complicated than it needed to be? Probably a generational thing. She glanced back at the word "priceless." Hopefully that didn't imply "without a price, not valuable."

But don't look past the cracks in the mortar.

The stairstep lines between the stones? There were plenty of cracks in the mortar between the stones in the fireplace. She needed to take a closer look.

Lest you miss the one you can wiggle and glide.

The loose one that had recently found its way onto the list of repairs? Though not very high on the list, it had just worked its way higher—at least to take a look at what might be behind it.

Although she would love to have headed straight to the drawing room, she couldn't allow the treasure hunt to take precedence over all her guests.

Tucking the diary with its newfound page safely back into the chest, she hoped to be able to examine the fireplace surround at some point soon.

CHAPTER TWENTY-THREE

The clanging of the front desk phone startled Elizabeth from her thoughts. Rashelle didn't seem to be within earshot, so she picked it up.

"Pennington Point Inn. This is Elizabeth. How may I help you?"

"Well, don't you sound so professional. Didn't expect *you* to answer the phone."

"Lucretia, how are you? So good to hear from you." Images from the previous summer of a weekend wedding gone terribly wrong flooded her mind.

"I'm okay. How are things with you? You've reopened the inn?"

"Yeah, finally got it open. Still more renovations yet to be completed. You know how it goes. Nothing is ever done on time. It's so frustrating. But at least we were able to open a good number of the rooms. And it's very exciting to have the new building with the fitness center in it . . . and the spa. The guests really seem to be enjoying the new amenities." Elizabeth found herself exaggerating a tad. She was confident they *would* be enjoying them but didn't have firsthand knowledge of any such merriment. Lucretia, with her own inn up the coast, didn't need to know any differently. Was she the competition? In a sense, she was.

"Great to hear. But I don't think I received my invite to the grand opening."

Elizabeth ignored the dig. "Haven't planned one yet. More likely it will be in the fall when everything is finished." Good God, the last thing she had time to worry about was a party of sorts. Or was she missing out on a unique promotional opportunity? She'd have to give that some thought. Kurt's stinging words that she was spreading herself too thin resurfaced. Perhaps she could delegate it to her day manager.

"I look forward to it. Lizzi, I wish you all the best with Pennington Point Inn."

"Thanks, Lucretia. I appreciate that."

"Lucy, please."

There was a pause during which Elizabeth pondered the reason for the call. Finally her friend began to fill in the blank.

"Liz, I needed to give you a call this morning, not just to wish you well with the inn, but because there's something I need to caution you about."

Leaning back on her heels, Elizabeth took offense at the implication she needed any guidance in running her family's inn.

"There still may be a threat lingering from the events that happened here last summer."

"Oh my God. What do you mean?" It couldn't be happening again—or still.

"I'm afraid Jonathon may still be alive."

Elizabeth couldn't form words. Her body stiffened.

There was shuffling on the other end. "Are you still there?"

"Yes . . . but how is that possible?"

"I don't know. The chief called last night to let me know there'd been reported sightings."

"Sightings?"

"Yeah, apparently he's been spotted a few times in the area. They've assigned an officer to protect me, which I hate. I mean, how does that look to our guests? I told him to stay out of sight."

Elizabeth dropped into the desk chair, grabbing on to the arms for stability.

"And his car . . . it seems to have disappeared."

"Disappeared?"

"Yeah. It's no longer at the far end of the front lot where it's been sitting since—"

She didn't have to finish. Elizabeth had been there to see firsthand the trail of carnage left behind by Jonathon Sterling.

"What kind of car?" She should at least know what to be on the lookout for on her end.

"Land Rover. Black."

"Okay."

"I just thought you should know."

"Of course . . . and I appreciate that."

"I'm sorry, Lizzi. I'm terrified on this end as well."

"I'm sure you are. I'm sorry, too. . . . So you said his car is black?"

"Yes."

"And isn't yours white?"

"Yes."

"Of course, it is. So fitting."

Lucretia gushed. "Guess so."

"All right. Please stay in touch. Let me know if you hear anything else."

"And you let me know if he turns up on your end."

Elizabeth let slip an unladylike snort and prayed *please keep him away from here. Throw him under a bus if you have to, but please keep him away.* A chill rippled through her body. Was her friend's husband—who had been missing and presumed dead—alive and well and eluding capture? Would he find his way to Pennington Point to come after her? He'd already killed a young man in a jealous fit of rage due to a tragic misunderstanding, and then Lucretia's childhood friend in an act that could only be described as grisly. What was to stop him from eliminating a more recent pal, all in the name of getting back at Lucretia? She'd have to clue in the deputy and perhaps consider hiring security for the inn. It hadn't been in the budget, but circumstances might be changing.

She twisted her hair between her fingers, running her thumb across the smooth strands, over and over, a nervous habit she'd developed since . . . since she left The Inn at Boothbay the previous summer with a killer on the loose? Since she took over at the helm of Pennington Point Inn? Hard to say. She found comfort in it, but tried to conceal her odd habit by turning away or doing it slowly.

Jonathon couldn't possibly still be alive. Could he? He would have had to survive a jump off the back of a moving boat, fully clothed in a business suit with wing-tipped shoes, and a swim to shore. If he'd made it that far, who would he have connected with to help him hide from the authorities? His brother was in custody the last time she was there. Had he gotten out?

She intended to hang on more tightly to Kurt when he was around.

Animated laughter and playful shouts drew her attention to the bar. Curiosity led her across the lobby to see the raucous group who was feeling no pain. When she reached the doorway, she grinned. It was their famous country star with his entourage. But things were clearly getting out of hand, and the bartender had lost control. Elizabeth strode toward Eli, hoping to talk some sense into him. He and his group needed to break it up or at least move the party into their rooms—of course, that came with the risk of disturbing Mrs. L.

She slid up behind him and ran her fingers down his back. When he spun around with a glass in hand, brown liquid sloshed out, and she had to take a step back to avoid getting splashed. His face lit up when he recognized her.

"Elizabeth, there you are. I was hoping you'd stop by. Why don't you join us?" Reaching for her hand, he wavered when he stood to greet her, and his words were slurred. The strong smell of whiskey accosted her nose when he kissed her cheek. She surveyed the group but didn't see his manager among them.

"That's very generous of you to offer, but I need to pass. And given the late hour, I need to ask that you and your friends head back to your rooms." The hour wasn't terribly late, but Eli probably had no idea, and they'd clearly had plenty to warrant a sendoff to bed.

"Oh, you can't be serious. We're just getting started." He squeezed her hand more firmly.

"Well, up here in Maine we tend to roll up the sidewalks earlier than—I would imagine—places you're used to staying in. I also have the other guests to worry about."

"They can join us." He gestured with a flourish to the empty tables.

"Eli, I don't see anyone lined up, hoping to do that. Like I say, it's an early-to-bed crowd here." As she glanced toward the lobby, a forty-something couple paused to take a look. Elizabeth silently urged them to keep moving and not step into the bar.

"Oh, c'mon, Elizabeth. Where's your party attitude?" His Australian accent was so enticing, she could listen to him talk into the wee hours.

"Guess I left it behind the registration desk."

"Don't you want your guests to be happy?" Drawn in by the glint in his crystal-blue eyes, she averted hers but felt her face flush.

The sound of the voice behind her made her jolt and pull her hand from Eli's. "Not at the expense of the other guests. I'm afraid you and your group will have to break things up." Kurt's voice was firm.

Eli ran his eyes up and down, evaluating his adversary, and shrunk back. Considering Kurt's words, he paused and then asked, "So who might I have the pleasure of speaking with?"

"Kurt Mitchell." He extended his hand, and they shook.

Stepping in to smooth things over, Elizabeth added, "Kurt and I run the Pennington Point Inn together." He slipped an arm around her waist as if to establish their personal relationship for Eli to see.

"Well, good tuh meet chew." He ran his fingers through his hair and glanced at the others who were watching the intervention unfold. "Guess we'll have to take it somewhere else, boys."

Grumbling over the sound of chairs scraping across the wood floor, the guys got up and shuffled out, leaving behind an array of beer bottles and cocktail glasses. At the doorway, Eli turned back and gave her a grin. "Good night, love. Another time, then." He raised his glass in the air and walked out with it.

CHAPTER TWENTY-FOUR

"*Lizzi, we might have a* problem with the chef." Kurt set his coffee mug on the counter with a dull thud and motioned for her to join him in the drawing room.

"What do you mean?" She'd had mixed feelings about hiring him in the first place. It was the last job to be filled. With such a pivotal position, she'd intended to take her time and be purposefully picky. But without a large pool to choose from and the grand reopening date set, she'd run out of time.

God, she missed Tony, the multi-talented chef during her grandmother's reign. Having garnered impressive accolades over the years, earning the respect of those in the gastronomy world and beyond, Tony was a tremendous asset to the inn. Amelia had counted on his expertise, not only in running a shipshape kitchen, but also in turning out consistent five-star meals. They'd been blessed to have him at the helm for nearly twenty-five years, unheard of in his line of work. It was a huge loss when Elizabeth wasn't able to hire him back. After the inn closed with no definitive timeline to rebuild, another highly acclaimed inn farther up the coast scooped him up, so he was not in a position to jump ship and return to Pennington Point when it finally reopened. He felt obligated to stay. And it wasn't that she hadn't tried to lure him away. Lord knew she'd embarrassed herself with her groveling. But while she'd respected his commitment to his new employer, Elizabeth had had no choice but to hire someone else.

"One of his references we weren't able to check out in the hiring process has turned up dead." Kurt waited for that to sink in as he plopped into a chair by the front windows. "Apparently Sam got a call this morning from a private investigator. The two were known to have business dealings in the past. I'm sure it didn't take them long to figure out where Vincenzo ended up when he left Las Vegas."

"But that doesn't necessarily mean . . . how can they be so sure there's a connection?"

"Well, they haven't been able to make a definitive connection as of yet, but they're looking into it."

"So, we don't have to jump to conclusions, do we?" Elizabeth remained on her feet, leaning against the chair across from him.

His serious features melted into his trademark crooked smirk. "Ah, Lizzi. Always the optimist. I love you for that."

She didn't care for the hint of condescendence and pushed back. "Are you kidding, I *have* to think that way. I never would have taken on the gargantuan task of reopening this inn—or anything else I've tackled in my life—without it."

"Look, this is where I have more experience than I care to remember." Unfolding his six-foot frame from the chair, his size underscored his authority on the subject. He turned toward the windows as if his escape from the latest snag lay somewhere out on the water. The burden of his memories as an agent seemed to hold him in an impenetrable vice grip. "Something as innocuous as not being able to reach someone has a way of turning into the missing piece that can break a case wide open." He smacked his palm against the top of the wingback. "I'm kicking myself now for not following through on that, not doing what I knew was the right thing. I didn't listen to my instincts. And in my line of work, you could lose your life with a mistake like that. I've seen agents killed for—" He wasn't willing to continue.

She crept nearer so she could speak softly. "Okay. I hear you. You're absolutely right. But I need to take responsibility for this as well. I was rushed at the end, trying to get everything done that absolutely had to be done before the reopening. But that should have been a red flag for me, too." She regretted her initial reaction to his revelation about their chef and not deferring to Kurt's expertise. "I just didn't want to hear another piece of bad news that could affect this place. I really want to make this work. I *have* to." Her thoughts caromed between the design career she'd all but abandoned and her responsibility as the sole surviving Pennington to carry on at the inn.

He turned and enveloped her in his strong arms, pulling her in. "Hopefully we'll find out this has nothing to do with our chef."

"Hope so." She also hoped he wasn't trying to convince himself.

"We've just got to be on the same page. Gotta go." He kissed the top of her head and headed out, leaving her to wonder what was so important he couldn't linger with her a little longer.

CHAPTER TWENTY-FIVE

Her *return trip to* Connecticut got drawn out to two days instead of one due to delivery delays and selections that didn't work once they were in place. Was she losing her touch? She was mortified to have to tell one very impatient woman who wanted the redo done before it was realistically possible that they'd have to place another order for a couch and matching side chair. Surely the manufacturer had made an error on the fabric they'd used. Out of view of her client, she cross-checked the shipping document with her notes from their consultation and found she was the one who'd made the costly and time-consuming error. And the cost was not only a hit to her pocket, but a gouge to her reputation.

Concerns with unhappy clients and unfinished projects made for a long ride back to Pennington Point. And she was none too disappointed to return Kurt's pickup to him. Unlike her Jeep, which was still out of commission and in need of serious bodywork, his truck drove like a—truck.

Once on the access road, the briny air that fluttered in through her cracked window helped push her worries to the side. Elizabeth was back home and would handle her clients' issues in due time.

At first sight of the flashing lights, she yanked her foot off the gas, coasting to a stop. A patrol car and an ambulance were parked on the circle, blocking the steps to the inn.

She pulled in a scant puff of air. "Oh dear God, what's going on now?" Her thoughts went to the guests but quickly reverted to Kurt. "Lord, no."

Rounding the circular drive, she pulled behind the ambulance and shut down the engine, bolting for the door. Once inside, she sidestepped to avoid getting bowled over by a pair of EMTs with a gurney between them barreling toward the exit, the wheels rattling over the threshold. All she was able to discern about the patient on its way by was brown hair. She decided the face looked masculine but quite pale. One of the guests?

Before long, Kurt appeared with the deputy behind him. Neither looked happy to see her. *What had she walked into?* Relieved the body on the way to the hospital or the morgue wasn't the man in her life, she looked to them for an explanation, but the deputy brushed past her, following the EMTs.

"What's going on? Who was that?" She flung her hand toward the screen door as it slammed shut.

Kurt took a moment, as if considering how to deliver the news. "That was our chef."

"It was? What the—what happened?"

"Not sure yet. His assistant came back after delivering a room service order and found him on the floor of the kitchen. Poor guy's pretty shook up."

Elizabeth flashed back to the body she'd tripped over a couple years earlier when all the trouble started at the inn. Flicking aside an errant lock, she endeavored to refocus on the present.

"Is he going to be okay?" She choked on her words.

"I'm no expert, but I *have* seen a few dead bodies in my time. If this one wasn't deceased yet . . . it didn't look promising."

The twinge in her abdomen was all too familiar. Could it be happening again?

CHAPTER TWENTY-SIX

Aside from the obvious—another untimely death at Pennington Point—they also had no one to run the kitchen. The young guy who had been Vincenzo's assistant didn't have the background or experience to be called so much as a sous-chef, so he couldn't be expected to fill a chef's shoes, in spite of their dire circumstances.

Kurt abandoned his nearly full glass of Cabernet on the small table between them, as if he'd suddenly lost interest in it, and leaned back into the chair.

Elizabeth tossed out the question they'd been mulling over in their heads while she clutched her glass. "So what do we do? . . . God, am I being overly crass talking about this before his body has a chance to cool off in the morgue?"

"You're a smart businesswoman who knows tough decisions have to be made, even in delicate situations like this. You also know your decisions affect many more people than just us."

Elizabeth recalled the sting upon learning the ripple effect of her leaving the inn in shambles for so long. The negative impact spread throughout her beloved hometown.

Kurt kept them on task. "In the short term, we'll need to provide guests with food since Sam has ordered everyone to stay put until he can get a chance to interview them. So we may have to make arrangements with other inns and hotels—"

"I can't get prepared meals from other inns. They're our competition. Word will get out that—"

"Okay, maybe not the inns. How about area restaurants?"

Elizabeth considered his suggestion. "Okay. We could do that. We'll put out a continental breakfast in the morning. I'll get meat and cheese platters with rolls for lunch. Maybe I'll whip up a soup each day, too."

"Soup?"

"Yeah. I make some great soups. You'll see."

"I look forward to it." He grinned at her defensive stance.

"So then we would just have to bring in dinner each night. Hopefully that won't last too long."

"All right. Good. Sounds like a plan."

"So what do we do long term? Shut down the inn while we search for another chef? I honestly don't think we could survive another closure, but I think potential guests would overlook us and make reservations elsewhere if there was no restaurant on-site. And the employees. If we shut down for a while, they'd probably leave and find other employment—not that I'd blame them—and wouldn't be available when we reopened. Kurt, I'm afraid we're doomed. God, it feels like someone is setting us up to fail." She ran her teeth across her lower lip. "Do you think that's possible?"

"Anyone come to mind?" He glared his condescendence.

"Well, there's Drescher to start with." Her former client's antics at the prior inn, the least of which could be construed as sabotage, landed him in prison.

Kurt nodded. "Isn't he still doing time?"

"Yeah, but I'm sure he's got cronies on the outside who could do the dirty work for him."

"What about Sterling?"

She had to admit he was a possibility, too. The unknown whereabouts of her friend's tyrannical husband, who was wanted for murder, had made it clear he had a vengeful distaste for Elizabeth.

"How about your old boss?"

"Vera? Nah. She doesn't have it in her. What about you? I bet there are plenty of characters lurking in your past that could resurface." Switching the focus, she was eager to at least share culpability.

A painful grimace appeared on his face but quickly slipped away. "Yeah, that's certainly a possibility."

"The difference is, I have no idea who you've nabbed and put behind bars only to have them get released again. At least *I* know who I've crossed paths with and need to be on the lookout for. How many are so pissed off they'd come after you to get revenge?"

He left the question unanswered, as though he couldn't begin to count the number. The thought terrified Elizabeth. What had she gotten herself into, falling in love with a former agent? Were they in imminent danger because of him? Could Kurt protect them?

Her pup stirred at her feet, reminding her he was still there. She leaned down and stroked the soft, warm fur on his head. Buddy certainly wasn't much of a guard dog. Didn't have the right temperament. That was part of the reason she'd been able to adopt him after he flunked out of police dog training. He was a loveable marshmallow who would wag his tail at anyone, including intruders and would-be murderers.

"All right. This is all so frightening to think about. Why don't we just keep moving forward and try to focus on what it would take to keep the inn running."

"Sounds reasonable." His voice was quiet and his face rigid. "And I'll contact the Bureau to see what I can find out—if there are any developments I should be aware of."

"Okay. Thanks." Relieved she could leave the messy security issues in his hands, Elizabeth returned to what she could wrap her head around. "So do we keep going and keep the inn open? We can use the excuse of an ongoing investigation to keep the kitchen closed for a while, but where do we go from there? Ask Vincenzo's assistant to step up and take on more responsibility? Though that's a scary thought. Could you and I try to give him a hand in the kitchen?"

Kurt snorted. "Seriously, Liz? That would be a joke—worse, a disaster. Maybe *you* could do it, but I have no business setting foot in a kitchen, certainly not a professional one."

"And what about the clambake we've been advertising?" She ignored his self-deprecating comment. "How do we pull that off? There's really only one person I know of who should attempt that, and he's—"

A familiar voice piped in from the foyer. "I think I can help you with that."

As Tony crossed the sitting room, Elizabeth jumped from her chair and met him halfway, throwing her arms around him.

"What are you doing here? It's so good to see you," she gushed.

Kurt rose and extended his hand to the new arrival.

"I've returned to take back my kitchen."

"Are you serious? You've returned? You can start working right away?" Elizabeth was ecstatic to see the former inn's seasoned head chef.

Tony nodded with a broad grin plastered across his face framed with graying wavy hair. Clearly he was happy to be back.

"You're a godsend. How did you know we needed you?"

"You'd probably be surprised how small the culinary world really is." Placing a gentle hand on her shoulder, he added, "Besides, I watch the news." He winked at Kurt.

"Well, I'm thrilled. You came at the right time. We were contemplating closing down the place again so we could search for a new chef. Your timing is perfect. I can't believe it. But now, what happened to your previous job?"

He grew more serious. "Let's just say my employer and I didn't have a meeting of the minds, so to speak. I heard you were in need of a head chef, so it made sense for me to make my move."

"Glad it worked out," Kurt chimed in.

"Yeah, I put in a couple years and gave it my best shot with the guy, but it just wasn't meant to be. In hindsight, I'm glad it didn't work out there. Couldn't wait to come back." He glanced around the room. "And I love the renovations you've done. Can't wait to see the rest of it. What does my kitchen look like? You didn't change that around, did you?" he ribbed.

"No. It's exactly the way you remember it. I knew the setup was perfect the way you had it, so I only cleaned it up and had it painted." Buddy leaned up against her leg as if looking for an introduction. "Oh, and you haven't met my furry sidekick. This is Buddy."

Tony let him sniff his hand before stroking his head and back. "Nice pup. I think we'll get along just fine . . . become good friends."

"I'm sure you will. As soon as he figures out what a great cook you are." They all shared a laugh.

Reeling from the unexpected good fortune, she felt blessed to be walking her favorite chef back to his kitchen to reacquaint him. Things had finally taken a turn toward a more positive outlook. But was it to last? Time would tell if they would be able to weather the blow to the inn's reputation of suffering yet another untimely death.

CHAPTER TWENTY-SEVEN

Torn between having to leave the inn in the hands of someone other than herself and missing the opportunity to meet Kurt's parents, Elizabeth decided the latter would have far more potentially regretful ramifications, so she opted to accompany him on his visit. She'd been feeling the mounting pressures of running the inn during a murder investigation and embraced the opportunity for an out. A few hours away without guests or clients to worry about. She didn't wait for Sam to clear their excursion; she informed the reluctant deputy they'd be away from the inn for the day but available by cell.

After rising early and driving up the coast, they took the ferry out of Boothbay Harbor for the hour and a half ride. As the day warmed, it turned out to be blissfully bright, though cooler on the water. Not a cloud in the sky. No storms appeared imminent—at least not from a meteorological perspective—and the air was unusually calm, which was reflected in the surface of the ocean.

They joined fellow passengers along the railing on the starboard side as the boat pulled out of the harbor. Gulls swooped down across the bow as if discerning whether or not the vessel was a fishing boat. Disappointed, they didn't linger.

Halfway into their journey, the cool air forced Elizabeth to pull her jacket out of her tote, and Kurt scooted closer, guiding the sleeves up her arms from behind. Retreating inside the nearly deserted cabin, they plopped onto one of the benches near the windows. At times, he seemed to be immersed in thought and looked like he was about to say something but decided against it. She let it go. The constant vibrating rumble of the engine felt soothing, nearly lulling her to sleep. Her head landed quite naturally on his shoulder.

Suddenly he pulled his arm away, and she straightened up. "What's wrong?"

"Elizabeth, there's something you need to know—something I need to get off my chest if I'm going to be straight with you—and I have to do it before we get to the island."

"Okay." She hoped she'd be able to hear him over the noise of the toiling engine.

His gaze wandered toward the windows, out to the open sea. She allowed him the time he needed to gather his thoughts.

"I left out an important detail about what happened to my brother."

"Okay, I'm listening." She didn't dare touch his hand or lay hers on his leg. He seemed to need to distance himself from her, to say what was on his mind.

"So that awful day—that I've wished every day of my life I could get back again—I was hanging out with my buddies, and

Jamie was hanging with us. I remember the guys were being great about taking turns to entertain him, and he seemed to be having a lot of fun. One of the guys had his skateboard with him and Jamie got on it." His voice softened. "He got on it and tried to do what the big guys had been doing. He got going down the sidewalk—it wasn't that much of a decline—but he was out of control before anyone could catch up to him." Kurt's eyes glazed over, no longer seeing what was in front of them. "I'll never forget the sickening thud when he hit the tree."

Unable to hold it in, she wiped a tear that burned on her cheek.

"My parents blamed me for the accident. I was supposed to be watching him. It was my responsibility, and I'd failed them—failed my brother."

"I'm so sorry." Searching for something more comforting than that, she blurted out her next thought. "Surely, there was nothing you could have done to prevent it. I bet it all happened very quickly."

He nodded.

"Your parents probably understand that. Maybe you're just being too hard on yourself."

"No. I deserve every ounce of guilt that I feel."

She hated to hear him condemn himself to a life of torture. Surely his parents had come to terms with the accident and saw it as just that. "Have you tried talking to them about it?"

He remained silent. At that moment, a young boy, about seven or eight years old, holding the hand of what looked like his father, brushed past Kurt, disturbing his daze. As he looked up, the boy turned back and smiled. Kurt blinked hard to hold off welling tears. While still focused on the boy climbing the stairs to the upper lever, he pulled his wallet from his back pocket and flipped it open. There, on his lap was the smiling, impish face of a boy who looked remarkably similar to the passerby.

"This is Jamie."

She knew before he uttered his name, but she acknowledged it anyway.

Elizabeth scooted closer. "He's adorable. What a sweet little boy. I bet he was a delight to be with." She recognized the dimpled grin that gave his big brother the same impish look. "Kurt, you should try talking to your parents. You've all been through hell because of this tragedy—which was an accident—and it could do all of you good if you worked through it. It could bring you closer."

"Well, I don't know about that, but I *was* planning to talk to them while we were here. I thought you should hear about it from my perspective first."

"I appreciate that." She took his hand. "I'm with you on this. We'll get through it together." He slid his other hand onto her thigh. She prayed his encounter with his parents could be part of a healing process for each of them.

Her hopes of bringing up the topic of the fiancée's letter on their return trip were dashed again. She couldn't possibly pile on more than Kurt was dealing with already.

Up the hill from the dock where the ferry had let them off, Island Inn sat prominently looking out over the water, appearing larger than she remembered. It was by far the grandest building on the spit of land.

The climb was steep. Elizabeth hung on to Kurt's arm. He was so strong, it felt as though he was pulling her up the hill on his own.

"So let me ask you something. Do your parents know I'm showing up with you today?"

His arm seemed to stiffen and his blinking became comically exaggerated.

"Do you think I should have told them?" He kept his focus forward.

Elizabeth stopped in her tracks, yanking him to a standstill, but he didn't turn to her. Soon his signature smirk spread far enough she could see it from the side.

"Oh Kurt Mitchell, you send me over the edge sometimes." She took a swipe at his upper arm, and they resumed their trek up the hill.

"Of course, I told them. They can't wait to meet you."

She took comfort in his words but hoped the unsettled sensation in her stomach was due to nervousness before meeting his parents and not her instincts telling her he wasn't being forthright.

At the top of the hill, he steered her to the left, and they headed up the narrow dirt road. Her head pivoted back and forth as she took in the familiar, quaint cottages and galleries along the way. Before long, he opened the gate of a white picket fence that defined a small yard bursting with hydrangeas and day lilies. She pulled up short, not expecting to be stopping so soon.

"This is it. My parents' cottage." He gestured with his free hand.

"It's beautiful. And they're so fortunate to be close to the dock . . . close to the general store along the road there."

"Well, let's go on in and—"

"There you are," came a voice from across the yard. A middle-aged woman with graying shoulder-length hair appeared at the front door. She beamed at her visitors. "I told your father I'd heard the boat. Right on time." Poking her head back inside, she called, "David, they're here." She sounded giddy.

Elizabeth was relieved to hear she'd been expecting the two of them, not just her son. Was part of his reason for bringing her along to soften his parents' reception to him?

As his mother skipped down the two front steps, his father took her place on the stoop, looking very much like a college professor with a wooden pipe pinched between his teeth. However, he didn't share his wife's exuberance. Cradling a mug in both hands, he surveyed the recent arrivals with guarded interest and shoved a hand in his pocket.

Acknowledging his father, Kurt called over with a raised hand, "Hey, Dad." He held up on a stepping-stone with a hand clutching Elizabeth's forearm. His mother rapidly closed in. "Hey, Mom." He beamed as she neared.

With outstretched arms, she gushed, "You must be Elizabeth. I'm Lillian. Oh, but you can call me Lil." She thrust her arms around her son's companion and squeezed. Elizabeth held her breath so as not to break the connection. Finally his mother pulled away. "So good to meet you." She turned to Kurt and showered him with the same welcome. She held on even longer, as though afraid to let go.

Slightly flushed, Kurt motioned to Elizabeth. "Mom, this is the lovely lady I've been telling you about."

Elizabeth finally found a chance to jump in. "So nice to meet you. What a lovely place you have. And your gardens are absolutely beautiful."

With a swat at the air, Lil fended off the compliments. "Oh, you're too kind. But I have to have something to paint if I don't feel like making the climb to the light." She chuckled to herself. "So come on in. I've made tea. You must be hungry."

They made their way to the front door where David stood firmly at his post. Kurt repeated the introductions which, this time, were less amorous, yet still cordial. Without a word, David held open the screen door and silently ushered their visitors inside. At the top of the steps, Elizabeth glanced back across the meticulously manicured yard and caught a stunning view of the lighthouse on the bluff. She understood how inspiring the location was for the artists and writers who flocked there. She imagined most didn't bring the baggage the Mitchells had carted with them.

Once inside, Elizabeth's eyes were drawn straight through the open layout of the modest home to the wall of windows along the back with breathtaking views of the ocean. Although she'd grown up with similar views on Pennington Point, she never tired of them.

Apologizing for the smoke that lingered in the air, Lillian grumbled something about how she'd hoped they could smell the blueberry muffins she had just pulled out of the oven. David grunted at his wife's comment and followed the group into the house, letting the door click shut behind him. Elizabeth assured her she didn't mind at all. There was a sweetness to the pipe's aroma that seemed to make up for the smoker's crusty disposition.

They enjoyed tea, coffee, and muffins in the sitting area in front of the windows. A couch and two small upholstered chairs were arranged in a u-shape, allowing everyone an ocean view. After pleasantries were exchanged, Kurt's parents asked about the renovations at the inn, so Elizabeth was able to share with them the lengths required to fix it up and how pleased she was to finally reopen her family's property. She asked his parents about the island and how it had been to endure their first winter there. They both chimed in and seemed to be genuinely happy about their time on the island so far. No one mentioned the couple's life before Monhegan, and Elizabeth wasn't going to be the one to bring it up.

"Well, that was lovely. Thanks so much for the coffee and scrumptious snack. I think I'll head out for a hike so I can burn off that second muffin." As she rose, Lillian's face fell, and David regarded her as if trying to discern an ulterior motive. "I'm sure you and Kurt have plenty to catch up on."

Lillian's head swiveled to Kurt, back to Elizabeth, returning to her son again. "Well, at least go with her. We wouldn't want her to get lost on the trails."

"I'll be fine. Really."

Kurt jumped in. "Yeah, she's been here plenty of times. Knows it better than I do. Lot of good I would be. Probably get us lost. Besides, I wouldn't mind a little time just the three of us." His father shot him a pained look as though he feared what was behind his words.

Lillian walked Elizabeth to the door while laying out directions to the nearest wooden box that contained maps of the island and cautioned her about the need for bug spray and sunblock, but Elizabeth assured her she'd be fine on all three accounts. With a supportive smile for Kurt, she slipped out the door, made her way onto the dirt road, and headed up to the lighthouse.

Draining the coffee pot to refill their mugs, Lillian settled into her chair and fell silent. Kurt hung his head, feeling the weight of his desire to clear the air, hoping to move on. It felt awkwardly staged. Finally, his father spoke first.

"What's on your mind, son? Looks like you've got something you need to talk about. . . . This visit isn't just for us to meet Elizabeth, is it?"

Kurt straightened up. "That's a big part of it."

"Do you intend to marry her?" His father fished his pipe from the ashtray and busied himself with cleaning it.

His mother placed a hand on her lips, half-heartedly stifling a gasp. "Are you?"

Smirking, Kurt nodded. "At some point, yes. I do hope to."

Lillian squealed and clasped her hands together. "Oh, that's wonderful, Kurt. She seems delightful. I'd love to get to know her better."

"But that's not why we're here today."

Unable to let it go as a simple jovial disclosure, David pressed, "Is she aware of your plans? Does she feel the same way?"

"Dad . . . I don't know yet. We've grown very close, and I can't imagine the rest of my life without her. I hope she feels the same way, but I haven't broached the topic yet. She's got a lot going on right now. She's had a lot to try to recover from in her life."

With a grunt, his father tossed the pipe back into the ashtray and grumbled, "She's not alone in that."

Kurt drew in a lungful of stale cottage air and let it out. This was his opportunity—staged or not—and he had no choice but to go for it. "I need to talk to you guys about what happened to Jamie—James."

His father grabbed his pipe again and became more earnest in preparing it to smoke, getting it just so. Lillian's words were barely audible. "What about it?"

Was she past talking? Was he dredging up painful memories they would rather leave undisturbed? Maybe. But he needed to bring them up one last time so *he* could move on.

"I don't know if this means anything to you, but I wanted to tell you how sorry I am about what happened." His words sounded flat and, worse, insincere. "A day doesn't go by that I haven't wished I could go back in time and prevent the horrible tragedy. I haven't stopped thinking about that day on campus. He was hanging out with us, happy as can be, and suddenly he grabbed the skateboard and took off, trying to be like the big boys. I couldn't get to him fast enough. We all yelled for him to stop, but he was in over his head. He didn't know what he was doing."

His mother covered her face with her hands, crying softly. Her petite body rocked back and forth.

David jerked forward in his chair. "Now look what you've done. You've upset your mother. Why did you have to go and bring that up again?"

"I need to talk about it once and for all—as adults. We really never did."

"Fine. You want to talk about it? Let's start with the fact that *you* had a responsibility. But you were spending more time with your friends than watching your brother that afternoon."

His mother came alive. "We don't know that, David. You're being too hard on him."

"Hard on him? I don't think so." He turned his anger toward her, jabbing the air with his pipe. "What I'm saying right now I think is ringing true to his ears."

"Oh, David, please. It's hurtful . . . and not productive. He's trying to bare his soul. Think about where he's coming from. He's living with this, too." She refocused on her son. "Kurt, please continue."

Without looking at his father, he kept going. "I never meant for Jamie to get hurt. I loved that little guy. He was my little buddy. We had a lot of fun together. Now, every day I look in the mirror and wish it had been me instead of him."

Lillian let out a low mournful sound. "Kurt, I wouldn't want it to be *either* one of you. Every day I ask God why I couldn't have both my boys alive." As her gaze wandered out to the horizon, David jumped in.

"See—see what this has done to your mother? It's just about killed her."

"David, please—"

Kurt sprang to his feet. "Look, I don't know what else I can say or how many times I can say it." He didn't try to hold back the thunder in his voice, furious at his father's inability to hear the sentiment behind his words. When he'd practiced his talk ahead of time and envisioned their reactions, this was his worst-case scenario. It sounded all too familiar.

His father was never going to forgive him. His gut told him to run, head out the front door, and leave him behind to wallow in his blame. He'd tried to make amends, and his father wouldn't listen. He'd drawn his conclusion years ago and had no intention of budging. Kurt yearned to go find Elizabeth and whisk her off the island, never to return. Carry on with his own life. The only glitch with that plan was the next boat didn't leave for another two hours.

Having wandered toward the front door, his back was to his parents. Petite arms embraced him from behind, startling him. His mother whispered, "Please come sit down again. Your father will . . . behave."

Almost amused by her choice of words, it was enough to break the tension and convince him to try again. He allowed her to take his hand and lead him back to the club chair next to the window. Then she took the lead.

"David, please try to hear what your son is sharing with you." She plopped down in her favorite spot next to her bag of knitting. "We've all been through a tragedy, and I *hate* the way it's torn us apart. We can pretend all we want that we're leading a normal life, and everything is just fine between us, but it's not. I'll admit, we ran away—which made it harder for you to come see us, Kurt." She studied the unfinished scarf sticking out of the bag before finding her son's hopeful face. "But that wasn't our intention. We were running from the excruciatingly painful loss. Getting as far away from campus as possible but still be in Maine was our way of doing that. But we've lost the family we had with the three of us. It barely exists anymore. There's no reason for that. It's not fair to you. James wouldn't want it like that."

David shifted in his chair and plucked his lighter from the ashtray, flicking on the flame and starting a new pipe. Soon a wisp of smoke wafted above his head, and the sweet aroma of tobacco filled the room. He remained quiet, and Kurt hoped he was listening.

Lillian continued. "Horrible things happen in life, even if we've done everything we could to prevent them. We'll never know why this happened to sweet little James. But we are in no position to be assigning blame for it." As though needing to veer off to a happier topic, she remembered, "He was such a sweetheart. Full of life. Could be a handful at times. And he had such an infectious laugh." She chuckled.

To Kurt's dismay, his father cleared his throat and took over with teeth clenched.

"When someone commits a wrong—especially an egregious act like this—it's imperative they take full responsibility for their actions."

He sounded more like the professor he used to be, holding court at the front of the classroom, than a father talking with his family.

"Apologizing is not the same as accepting responsibility. I want to hear that you accept responsibility for what you've done—not only to your baby brother but to this family. It's on *your* shoulders, and you need to—"

"*David*, you have no right to talk like that." Lillian gripped the endcaps on her chair.

"Oh, yes I do. He needs to hear this."

"How can you put the responsibility on him?"

"How can I? Because I have more information than you do."

"What are you talking about? You're not being fair," Kurt's mother pleaded.

"An eyewitness to the event approached me and told me what he saw. I was appalled at Kurt's actions that day."

"Who?" she demanded.

David ignored her question. "He told me how Kurt actually encouraged little James to get on the skateboard even though he seemed reluctant to try it."

Kurt couldn't remain quiet any longer. "I did no such thing."

"Well, I guess it's your word against his, isn't it? And, of course, you're going to deny it."

"David, who could possibly have said that to you? And why didn't you say anything to me before now?"

To Lillian's frantic questions, he replied simply, "I didn't want to cause you any more pain than you were going through. But now that Kurt has brought it up again, it became relevant."

"Tell me who. I want to know. I think you owe me that. Your son deserves to know as well." Her voice wavered with her last words.

"You don't need to know."

"You're willing to sit here and crucify your son based on one person's story who you're not willing to divulge?"

CHAPTER TWENTY-SEVEN

"He was a reliable source. One of the faculty. A respectable person."

Lillian wasn't backing down. "Who, *damn* it?" The sharpness of her voice caused her husband to flinch. "We all deserve to know. Kurt certainly deserves to know who his accuser is."

"All right, all right." He slammed the pipe into the ashtray, sending ashes scattering across the table. "It was Dan."

"Dan who?" she implored.

"Dan . . . Bernasky."

Lillian's eyes flared. "Bernasky—the same guy who was fired for lying during his interview and making false claims on his résumé?" She got to her feet. "Oh God, David. How could you have trusted him? He's nothing but a con and a—"

"Enough." He threw a hand up to silence his wife. "End of discussion, unless Kurt has anything else to add."

It had all turned out exactly as he'd feared, only worse. In his head, even though his father blamed him all those years, Kurt had envisioned being able to convince him to see his perspective for once. Defeated, he gave his mother a hug and a kiss on the side of her face and left. No one stopped him. No one came after him. Not even his mother. Had she taken his father's side? In his mind, choosing not to disagree was the same as agreeing. He guessed she needed to be able to live with him.

Letting the screen door slam behind him, he started up the hill to the lighthouse, passing couples and families on their way down, engaged in bubbly chatter. If anyone spoke to him, he didn't notice. At the top, he found Elizabeth on the bench looking out over the island and the ocean to the west. The air was particularly clear.

The view went on for miles. He slid next to her. Without a word, she wrapped a nurturing arm around his shoulders, and he leaned in. He was grateful she seemed to understand what he needed.

They passed the two hours up on the precipice in silence until they could see the boat approaching from the distance. Once it had tied up, they made their way down the hill, past the cottage with the white picket fence, down the ramp to the dock.

The ocean on the return trip to Boothbay Harbor was much choppier than the trip out, the effects of a storm well off the coast. With each rise and fall of the hull against the churned-up seas, a thunderous spray hit the expansive windows on the sides of the boat. The little boy from the morning boat ride sat a couple rows behind them, depositing the contents of his stomach somewhere it didn't belong. The sour stench wafted forward as he coughed intermittently and wailed on his father's lap.

Elizabeth fought to talk her own stomach out of joining in on the heaving. She'd spent countless hours out on the ocean over the years, never with a gastrointestinal issue to speak of. And this was no time to start. Searching for an out, a way to put some distance between them and the sobbing, she glanced around them. On a calm sea, the rows of benches on the upper deck would be nearing capacity, and the railing along the bow would be shoulder to shoulder with tourists eager to catch a glimpse of a dolphin or harbor seal. Today the inside cabin was standing room only, the passengers' faces etched with misery. It looked like others would be joining in on the retching shortly. There was nowhere for anyone to go.

The captain, up on the bridge with her back to the passengers, held fast to the wheel, peering through the windshield wipers' hypnotic back and forth movement, working in vain to keep a clear line of sight. Elizabeth tried to imagine her with a confident expression, not one of trepidation.

Slipping her hand onto Kurt's to remind him she was there, they rode out the rough seas in silence. His jaw visibly clenched; his thoughts were clearly still back on Monhegan.

With the sun dropping toward the horizon, an unwelcome chill crept into the air. Elizabeth's stomach was still out of sorts by the time they reached land, as much from the rhythm of the boat as her concern for Kurt. She feared the trip may have been the last time he would see his parents.

CHAPTER TWENTY-EIGHT

"Sam, *I need to speak with* you a moment." If she wasn't so angry at the deputy, she would have been amused by the way she'd made him jump. She strode toward him.

"Miss Pennington." He held his ground next to the squad car as she neared.

"What's this about the poor woman I found in the fitness center with a barbell wedged into her esophagus? Kurt tells me it may not have been an accident."

"That's correct. We're pursuing—"

"First of all, you come to me with anything that has to do with the inn."

"I'm sorry." He pulled back slightly, not having seen this side of her before. "I thought you and Kurt—"

"Don't be making any assumptions. You come to me. I'm your contact person here. Got that?" She pulled back her index finger poking the air like it wasn't sure where to go.

"Yes, ma'am. I'm sorry about—"

"Now, tell me what's happened. Why do you think it may not have been an accident? And if you don't think it was, what do you think—do you think she was murdered?" *Lord, please don't let it be happening again.*

"Well, let's not jump to any conclusions yet."

"What have you found out? What's going on?"

"I'm sorry, Miss Pennington. It's an ongoing investigation. I can't go into details."

"Obviously you told Kurt more than you're telling me."

"I think I may have mentioned we were looking into other possibilities, that's all. We have to pursue all viable leads, follow our hunches."

"What hunches?"

"I'm sorry, I can't."

"Look, my number one priority here is the welfare and safety of my guests." One, in particular, whose fans would miss him if he were gone, she mused. "Should I be concerned? Are they in danger?"

"No, I wouldn't say they're in danger." He sounded about as convincing as a fox telling a hen he'd simply stopped by to say hello.

"So can we lift the restriction on our guests leaving the inn?"

"Not quite yet. I've got a few more leads to follow up. I'll let you know."

Sam shifted his weight. "I'm glad you tracked me down. There's something I need to talk to you about."

"Okay."

"What, uh . . . what are the circumstances surrounding Tony's return?"

"What do you mean?" In her head, her dukes went up, ready to defend her chef.

"Elizabeth, wouldn't you say it's a little bit of a coincidence that he shows up right when you need him, after your current chef happens to turn up dead?"

"A coincidence? No, I would call that a godsend."

"That may be, but I find it pretty convenient that the head chef position opens up, and suddenly he arrives, ready to come to the rescue."

"It just worked out that way. He put in a couple years with the inn that took him on after Pennington Point closed. I think he was grateful for a job that wouldn't have been his first choice, but he was in a bit of a desperate situation. He couldn't be picky. I know he gave it his best shot, but he and his employer didn't exactly see eye to eye. If you ask me, they didn't know what they had. Certainly didn't appreciate him."

"While I understand your loyalty to a man who's been at the helm here longer than anyone—"

"Longer than anyone else and far superior as well. Do you know the awards he received while he was—"

"Elizabeth, let's bring it back in. I need to be more objective than that and look for motive."

"Motive?" She suppressed the urge to shove the deputy away from her. He was heading down the wrong path.

"Yes. Motive. We've got a dead chef, and I have to look at everyone who's here and all the possible motives. Tony's on the list."

"Everyone? I suppose I'm on the list, too."

"Of course."

CHAPTER TWENTY-NINE

Having *exhausted all* possible angles to convince the deputy otherwise, Elizabeth watched as he led their chef out the front door to the idling squad car. He couldn't be swayed to take Tony when he wasn't in the middle of preparing for the evening's dinner. A murder investigation took precedence. She understood that, but why not talk to him at the inn? She guessed the element of getting him out of his comfort zone was part of the process. Yet she needed him in the kitchen—in *his* kitchen. He was such as an asset there. Of all the people who'd lost their jobs after the hurricane, he was the one her heart broke for the most—and the one she desperately wanted back and would do almost anything to get him back. She was thrilled it seemed he felt the same way.

For an uncomfortable moment, Sam's words echoed in her head. Was there too much of coincidence with Tony's arrival so soon after Vincenzo was suddenly snuffed out? Could he possibly have taken matters into his own hands? Was there a connection between Tony and Vincenzo? He *did* say the culinary world was a small one.

Returning to her laptop, she began a search for the inn Tony had just departed from, a beautiful seaside establishment in the harbor town of Camden, up the coast beyond Boothbay Harbor. She scrolled through the articles, looking for news about the place—anything unusual. Harbor View Resort and Spa popped up a few times. There were the standard blurbs about booking ahead for your holiday party, making a reservation for Mother's Day brunch, and an enticing invite to a combination wine tasting/art exhibit opening. But one recent headline in particular caught her attention.

OWNER OF CAMDEN'S HARBOR VIEW RESORT FILES FOR BANKRUPTCY PROTECTION

Why hadn't Tony mentioned that part of the story? He must have known. The article was dated before he left. She skimmed the lines of text to learn they'd been in and out of bankruptcy court for years after the death of one of the owners who had allegedly taken on hundreds of thousands of dollars of debt with the inn as collateral, unbeknownst to his partner. Filing for bankruptcy seemed to be their only way out from under the weight of the loans.

Had Tony realized the extent of their financial perils and felt he had no choice but to get out before he was taken down with them? Whether he left on his own or stuck it out until the eventual demise of the inn, it still left him out on the street without a job. Did he panic and return to the place he knew best, only to find someone in his coveted position? Perhaps, but Elizabeth found it hard to believe her Tony could have been desperate enough to take the life of another man.

Was it possible he feared for his life in Camden? The article didn't mention the deceased owner's cause of death. It could simply have been from natural causes. Or at the hands of his partner who had lashed out at him after discovering the sizable debt. Her mind raced with possibilities.

Clicking the back arrow, she scanned farther down the list of articles, latching on to an earlier posting from a local paper. Although it was a ragtag publication that was considered more of a tabloid than a legitimate journal, people read it from cover to cover and believed every word.

CHEF OF LOCAL INN INVESTIGATED FOR SIPHONING FUNDS

"No," she whispered, praying it wasn't the Harbor View, only to find the name at the end of the opening sentence. Her eyes skipped across the words, searching for his name. There was no mention of the chef they were referring to, but it was no less damning. Her heart thudded in her chest. Could it be true? But why? She reminded herself the paper had a reputation for reporting rumors that hadn't been substantiated. Returning to the original list, she searched for another article that pointed to the failing inn's chef and didn't come up with one.

Her thoughts turned to Tony, hauled in for questioning at the sheriff's office. What could Sam be asking him? Was he aware of the siphoning allegations? A more pressing question: How long was he going to detain him? Had Sam already found something substantial that gave him cause to take Tony into custody? If so, how was she going to get along without her chef? Guests would be expecting dinner soon. If he was gone much longer, she was going to have to tie an apron around her waist and pick up where Tony had left off.

Like anyone could really do that.

CHAPTER THIRTY

The breeze off the water played with the bottom corners of Elizabeth's drawing pad. She had thought it would be inspiring to sit at the picnic table near the stairs to the beach, but she'd spent most of the preceding hour stressing over a murderer in their midst while the deputy had the wrong man in custody and, the more immediate concern, how the inn was going to manage without a chef—again. She'd produced neither sketches for her client nor a culinary solution.

Crunching of gravel pulled her thoughts out of the kitchen as she watched the squad car round the drive and pull up just beyond the stairs to the porch. Both front doors opened, and Deputy Austin exited the driver's seat while Tony got out on the opposite side and scampered up the steps.

Relieved her illustrious chef was back where he should be, Elizabeth waited for Sam to saunter over, past the boxwoods where the man had gone over the edge. She felt for the young couple, whose lives had been irrevocably changed by tragic events—at her inn. There were lingering questions she hoped Sam could put to rest at some point, though she wasn't entirely sure she wanted to know. Had the young husband attacked his wife in a jealous rage? Had they reached an end point in their marriage and he wanted out, but she wouldn't agree to a divorce? The "why" might be a moot point; the end result was the same.

With his sights set on the movement of his feet as he approached, he seemed to be gathering his thoughts—or postponing the inevitable. After a moment, he plunked down sideways across from her, swinging his legs over the bench in an awkward, jerking motion. Finally, he began.

"Thank God that was just a formality."

"So Tony's been cleared of being connected with any wrongdoing." Then she added, "Here at the inn." She wondered if Sam was aware of the goings-on in Camden and what Tony had been accused of. If not, she was not about to enlighten him. She needed her chef right where he was. Her conscience tugged at her, but she didn't relent. "He didn't murder anyone."

"It doesn't appear that way. No."

"You sound disappointed," she poked.

His expression turned sour. "'Course not."

She imagined he was more frustrated than disappointed. "Starting to get to you, Sam?"

"Get to me? You think I've hit a dead end with no leads to chase down? I'm just getting started. I'll get to the bottom of this before you know it. You'll see. I've got this covered."

"I know you do. I didn't mean to imply anything to the contrary." Eager to retrieve him from his defensive stance, she redirected. "So, any word on Mr. Chase?"

"As a matter of fact, yes. Miraculously, Mr. Chase's condition has been upgraded to serious, so we've been able to get in there and chat with him—only a few minutes at a time, but we've made the best of it."

Elizabeth pressed a hand to her chest. "That's so good to hear. I hope he continues to improve. After seeing him lying lifeless on the landing, I could only imagine . . ." She shook off the gruesome image.

The deputy nodded but remained tight-lipped for the moment. Finally, he started in on the details. "Turns out the young woman had been diagnosed with MS a few years ago, not long after they were married. They were both devastated, understandably; but when her condition started to rapidly deteriorate over the last several months, she insisted they make plans to end her life early. She wanted him to be able to go on with his life. At first the husband refused to go along with the idea, but she wouldn't give up, finally convincing him she would do it without his help; but this could be his last gift to her."

"How awful. I can't imagine being put in that situation. He was damned either way."

"No kidding. The plan was to have her overdose on a pain med so it was painless for her—"

"Yeah, but not for him."

"We figured he carried her to the fitness center and set her up to look like she broke her own neck when she dropped the weights. He had to have done it early in the morning so no one would notice."

Then it dawned on her. "I'm pretty sure they specifically requested a room in Moosehead."

"Figured as much."

"So he dropped the barbell on her neck?"

"He had to. But she was already gone at that point. There was no bruising on her neck to indicate her heart was still beating."

"Good God."

"Without any surveillance footage to work from, we're making some assumptions and drawing conclusions based on what evidence we have and our conversations with him."

"Well, I'm not about to add security cameras in the gym or anywhere else on the property. I don't think our clientele would appreciate—"

"We've covered that already, Elizabeth. I'm not suggesting you should. I'm just stating the fact that we're working within the parameters of the information we have."

She backed down. "Could the ME place the time of death?"

"Not precisely, but he did conclude she'd been gone for a while before you found her."

"Did the husband think no one would figure it out?"

"Probably thought a small town like this wouldn't have the facilities to do a proper autopsy."

Elizabeth thought of all the untimely deaths at the inn and wished the ME hadn't had so much practice.

"I bet he couldn't stand to live with himself for going along with her wishes."

"Could be. Of course, once we started asking questions, he knew we were onto him. He also knew he wouldn't be getting any insurance money. They don't pay out for suicide—including assisted suicide. And the couple had amassed a significant pile of medical bills that were way overdue. He would be buried for years trying to get out from under them."

Clearly, the man had not anticipated the stairway when he set out to self-inflict bodily harm. He'd been shooting for a spot much farther below. "He saw no other way out than making his own exit. I can't imagine the unbearable burden that was crushing him. The whole situation is tragic. I just wish the inn didn't have to play a role in it." She regretted he'd heard her words when she caught his side-glance but meant them.

CHAPTER THIRTY-ONE

nnouncing her arrival with a knock on the nearest counter to avoid startling Tony, Elizabeth eased the swinging door closed. It no longer had a voice, thanks to someone who must have grown tired of the incessant squeaking and threw oil on the hinges. Tony was engrossed in rinsing out a large lobster pot in the sink, which he let go of after catching sight of her over his shoulder. Snatching a corner of his apron's bottom edge, he dried his hands as his face lit up at the sight of her.

"Great to see you back, Tony."

"Great to *be* back, Elizabeth." In spite of his smile, his eyes held a dullness. She hadn't noticed when he first showed up, but his frame seemed smaller than she remembered. His face was thinner. His hair grayer. The two years away seemed to have taken more of a toll on him than one would have expected. She tried to assure herself even if she had begun renovations right away, he still wouldn't have been able to leave the Camden inn. She hated to broach the topic, but she had to.

"Tony, I need to talk to you."

"Sure thing. Have some menu ideas?"

"No. Nothing like that. I'll leave all that up to you. You're the expert there."

"I would welcome your suggestions. You know that, don't you?"

"Of course, but I also trust you implicitly." At least with the food. Could she trust him beyond the kitchen? "I need to ask you about your last job."

His face grew ashen as he shoved his hands into pockets. "What about it?"

Was she about to accuse her chef—a longtime family friend—of stealing? She didn't feel she had a choice. She had to know. She *deserved* to know.

"I've been . . . an article came to my attention about the Harbor View . . . about the financial problems . . . and the death of one of the owners."

"Yeah, that was a real mess."

"I can imagine. So the inappropriate actions weren't discovered until after his death?"

"Oh, I think Allan had his suspicions, but it all came to a head once he could get his hands on the books without Ed standing over him."

"How tragic for an historic inn like that to have its future put into jeopardy because of one misguided—perhaps greedy—individual."

"So true."

She hoped he was drawing a parallel and pressed on.

"An earlier article talked about—" Her pulmonary function shut down for a moment. "—the chef who apparently had his hand in the pot."

"The chef? Where'd you hear that, the *Journal Enquirer?*"

"Could be."

"That rag isn't worth the paper it's printed on. You can't trust what's written there. And then it ends up on the internet, so everybody believes it because it's in black and white."

"So you didn't engage in any illegal activity while you were there? I'm sorry, Tony, I have to ask."

"Even if the article was true . . ." His gaze dropped to the floor. "It wouldn't have been about me."

"What do you mean?"

He shifted his stance to lean against the sink and folded his arms.

"What do you mean, Tony? You were the chef."

"That's the point." His words seemed difficult to get out. "I wasn't."

She let the silence prompt him for more.

"And I don't believe I led you to think I was."

"So what did you do?" She found it hard to believe he would have taken a job as anything else—anything less.

"Elizabeth, I was desperate. I needed a job. I have a family to support. When the hurricane shut down the inn, no one was hiring chefs."

"But you have such a stellar reputation. You've earned awards over the years. Anyone should be begging you to work for them as the head chef."

"I appreciate that, Elizabeth, but no one needed a chef, so it didn't matter if I was Jacques Pépin."

"So what did you do?"

"I took what I could get. It was a hell of a drive each day and it got old real fast, but I had to take what I could get. It barely paid the bills, but I had no choice." His posture seemed to shrink as he spoke.

"What did you do?" She tried again, sensing the pain it was causing him to confess to her.

"I was a part-time sous-chef."

"Sous-chef." Hardly the position he should have commanded. To say he was overqualified was indisputable.

"Yeah, the idea was I was to start out as a sous-chef and prove myself and work my way up to chef. Then the other owner—not Allan who had hired me—brought in his son. Didn't seem to know the arrangement I had with Allan." He allowed himself to be distracted by his fingers as he ran them along the edge of the counter like he was admiring a new car. "Allan assured me our plan was still in place and also said he would throw in part ownership of the inn when I did become chef—with no cash outlay on my part. I believed him. And it was too good to pass up. So when you came around and dangled this place in front of my nose, I couldn't leave. There was too much at stake—or so I thought."

"I had no idea. I'm so sorry."

"Me, too. I finally woke up and realized it wasn't going to happen. I'd been a fool to believe all the promises. That's why I was so happy to see—I'm sorry to say—the demise of your chef."

Had he known Vincenzo? Elizabeth wondered how much of the story the authorities were aware of. "Did Sam know about all this?"

"He does now. . . . He did his homework and had plenty of questions for me—very pointed questions. But I think I satisfied him that I was clean."

"Tony, obviously I had no idea what you were going through. I'm so sorry—"

"Don't be. I consider it all an act of God. None of us could have predicted that—or have been prepared for it either. We all survived the hurricane but had to go through hell afterward to get back to where we wanted to be."

Elizabeth admired his tenacity to find work—even if that meant stooping to do what a brand-new culinary school grad would be expected to endure—in order to provide for his family. She could only imagine how humbling that was for him. To make matters worse, her year of indecision had had a far-reaching ripple effect that included Tony's family.

At that opportune moment, Buddy nosed into the kitchen and wagged his way over to the two of them, providing a welcome intrusion.

"There's my furry friend." Tony lunged for him and stroked his head and sides, putting his face close to the pup's. Buddy's tongue slid out and swiped Tony's nose, which produced a guttural laugh Elizabeth was relieved to hear. The pup sat back on his haunches, drinking in the attention.

"Well, you two have certainly grown close in the short time you've been back."

"Yup. He's a great guy."

Once Tony stopped petting him, Buddy slipped past them and stood with his nose at the door of the upright cooler.

"Oh, let me see what I've got for you, Bud." He pulled on the handle and fumbled inside for a moment before pulling out a small package wrapped in stiff white paper. "You might like one of these." Slipping out a morsel, he commanded the pup to sit and then give him his paw before rewarding him with a meatball leftover from the previous night's dinner.

Elizabeth watched in disbelief. "Tony, I didn't know he could do that. Did you train him?"

Licking his chops, looking for more, Buddy sat with his attention focused on his culinary friend.

"Yeah, turns out he's a quick learner." He pulled out another meatball. "Lie down." The pup obeyed, sliding to the floor with his eyes locked on Tony's. Again he was rewarded for his efforts. "Okay, Bud. That's it." Tony patted his hindquarter, which seemed to be the signal the session was over. Buddy popped up and headed for the door, nudging it enough to plow through.

After returning the leftovers to the fridge, Tony washed his hands in the sink, casting a wary eye toward Elizabeth. "I know. He really shouldn't be in here. But he seems to understand if no one is around and it's just me in here, he can get away with it. It's our special connection. It doesn't last long, but it's pretty cool.

Elizabeth decided to let it go. Tony knew how to run his kitchen. She was relieved to have him back. She hoped the authorities wouldn't dig deeper and uncover another reason to pull him out of there.

CHAPTER THIRTY-TWO

The rattle of his cell startled Kurt. On his way back through the woods, after inspecting the progress of the tennis courts, he didn't recognize the number at first. And then it hit him. It had been a while.

"Dad?"

"Yes, son, it's me."

Kurt's thoughts went straight to his mother, hoping the reason for the call wasn't for bad news. There'd been no communication since his visit with Elizabeth, and he honestly didn't expect there to be ever again.

"What's up?" His voice warbled, so he cleared his throat.

"Son . . . I called to apologize."

"Apologize?" He never saw that coming.

"Yeah. I wish this was in person, but I've got to get this off my chest. It can't wait."

Kurt found an overturned log to sit down on. Buddy sidled up next to him and lay down, flopping across his feet as if to let him know he was there for him.

"I've been wrong to place the blame for your brother's death on your shoulders. I was being completely unfair. Your mother finally got me to see what I was doing. I wanted someone else to blame besides myself."

Running his fingers through his hair, Kurt remained silent, allowing his father to run through his well-rehearsed dialogue. Buddy tugged at one of Kurt's shoelaces.

"All these years I've felt guilty for not spending more time with James, getting to know him better, being a real father to him, and my opportunity died with him. I was so wrapped up in teaching and becoming tenured and securing grants. . . . It was all-consuming. When I lost him, my chance of ever getting that time with him vanished. I wanted someone to blame. In my mind, you were it. But your mother got me to see a different perspective. And when I could see yours, I suddenly could see mine better. . . . I am so sorry. I was a terrible father to you, too. Instead of embracing you and cherishing every moment I could with the only son I had left, I put you in exile. I've been such a terrible father."

"You're not terrible," was all Kurt could manage, choking on his words.

"I'm not asking for you to forgive me. I certainly wouldn't blame you if you didn't. I just don't want you to go through the rest of your life thinking you were responsible. It was an accident. That's it. A horrible, horrible tragedy. But an accident."

"What about the eyewitness who came forward?" Kurt's voice was a raspy whisper.

"Oh, I never should have listened to him. He was a lying, no-good louse who was always looking to start trouble. I should have listened to you and all your friends who were right there when it happened. I thought they were all trying to keep you out of trouble—covering for you. I should have known they were telling the truth. They were good kids, like you."

His father's words were a long time in coming, and Kurt had never thought he'd ever hear them. Silence on the other end prompted him to respond, but he struggled to put words together.

"This means a great deal to me, Dad. I can't begin to tell you how much." He blinked away welling tears.

"We've all suffered from this tragic loss, and the only way we can move on is to accept that it was an accident. James wouldn't want us to keep going the way we've been living. We'd like you back in our lives, Kurt. And that special lady Elizabeth, too, if that's the direction you two are going."

They made plans to meet in Boothbay Harbor for lunch. His father had an appointment coming up, and his parents were going to spend the day to make it worth the trip out from Monhegan. Kurt hoped Elizabeth would go with him. He needed the distraction. But more importantly, he needed his parents to understand how important she was to him.

Buddy leaned against his leg and dragged his warm tongue across Kurt's hand, nuzzling under it. In return, he received a pat on his head and a stroke down his side.

A dog's life was so simple; he just had to ask for affection and, in the right household, he got it. For people, it was much more complicated; it wasn't always clear what it took to earn love and acceptance. And some people had to wait years to receive it. For others, it never came.

CHAPTER THIRTY-THREE

He *didn't have to ask.* Elizabeth wasn't going to miss tagging along on Kurt's rendezvous with his parents. She sensed he might need her support as he endeavored to rebuild his relationship with his father. At best, it had been tenuous for years, and more recently, tumultuous. The next steps each took were critical.

They settled into one side of a dark green vinyl booth along the windows that looked out over the harbor. Many of the boat slips were empty, owing to the noon hour with charters out for the day. The waitress dropped off four Lobstah Shack menus and a separate list of craft beers on a single sheet of white paper. She promised to return when the rest of their party arrived. Before long, she reappeared with dripping glasses of water, filled to the brim, and dropped them off with four clunks.

Kurt checked his watch for the third time since they'd sat down. It was uncharacteristic of his parents to be late. No words of concern were shared aloud. They busied themselves with the brief menu. After the waitress stopped by again to check on the status of the rest of their party, Elizabeth tried to put his mind at ease.

"Your father's appointment probably ran late."

Cocking his head, he pointed out, "Thirty minutes? I would have thought they would have called. They don't text, but they could certainly give me a call, so I wouldn't worry."

"Well, maybe they don't have cell service in whatever building they're in. Please don't worry—"

"—until there's something to worry about?"

Chuckling, she blushed. He knew her well. "I just hate to see you stressing over something that could be a non-issue."

Movement across the bustling restaurant caught their attention as David and Lillian made their way to the table. As they neared, their faces appeared drawn from the weight of an imperceptible burden that hadn't been there during Elizabeth and Kurt's visit on Monhegan.

"Hello, you two!" Lillian clasped her hands together while she waited for them to scoot out of the booth. David remained behind her without as much as a word, his lips pursed together. Elizabeth was scooped into her embrace first, and it lasted a tad longer than expected. Kurt's father's hug was more reserved but warm nonetheless.

No sooner had they settled back into the booth than the waitress swooped by to take their order. They sent her away with the promise of making their decisions by the time she returned.

The small eatery had filled up during their wait, and the din from the lunch crowd didn't lend itself to quiet conversation.

They eventually placed their order and worked their way through pleasantries until Kurt asked about the appointment.

Lillian took the lead. "I'm so sorry we kept you waiting. You know how doctors' offices can be sometimes. They get backed up, and they leave you sitting in the waiting room. You wonder if they've forgotten you."

"Oh, we hadn't been here long when you arrived," Elizabeth offered, endeavoring to put them at ease.

"What doctor's appointment?" Clearly news to Kurt, he brought them back on point.

"Just a follow-up." David dismissed the concern in his son's voice. "No biggie." Looking to drop the subject, David shot a side-glance to his wife. She pressed further.

"There was nothing routine about it. That's why we were late." She addressed him under her breath. "I think they should know."

With clenched jaw, Lillian's gaze wandered onto the dock and followed a toddler bouncing along the wharf clinging to her mother's down-stretched hand. When she turned back, she blinked forcefully and whispered, "Okay?" With a nod from her husband, she continued, filling them in on his annual physical appointment she'd had to convince him to keep, routine blood tests and subsequent scanning tests—with and without contrast—and the follow-up appointment that was their reason to make the trip out from the island that day. David listened as if she was talking about someone else, detached from the specifics.

"So what did they say today?" Kurt's voice was even, yet sounded unfamiliar to Elizabeth.

David chimed in, "Nothing is definite, and there are still tests to be done. Let's not start worrying unless there's truly a reason to."

Kurt's head tilted ever so slightly toward Elizabeth with the familiar message in his father's words. "What's going on, Dad? You can tell us. Quite frankly, you're scaring me."

With the mounting tension, Elizabeth would have traded her location with almost anywhere else, including the front desk of the inn.

At that awkward moment, the waitress arrived to deliver plates of piping-hot fried clams, a fish sandwich, and a couple lobster rolls piled high and spilling out of their cardboard sleeves, all accompanied by salty French fries. She leaned over to the table across the aisle to grab condiments and plunked them down.

The booth remained silent until she had stepped away, out of earshot, leaving them undisturbed for a while.

"I'm sorry we're scaring you, Kurt. I really didn't want to bring it up." He shot a glance to Lillian's half of the bench.

"They need to know," she fired back.

Feeling like she was eavesdropping on a very personal conversation, Elizabeth squirmed to the edge of the bench but couldn't scoot out since she was still penned in by Kurt. "Ya know, this really isn't my place to be sitting here. Let me step out for—"

"Nonsense, dear. There's no reason for you to do that. Besides, we're not going to carry on any longer. We're going to change the topic." His mother grabbed the ketchup and squirted a sizable puddle next to her fries that could have served the entire table.

With the serene water view lost on all, polite conversation wove its way in between bites. Elizabeth couldn't help feeling resentful for being used to avoid the sensitive topic.

The drive back to Pennington Point seemed longer than usual. Lizzi had wanted to suggest stopping in to see her friend Lucretia while they were in town but thought better of it. Another time.

What was left unsaid at the lunch table became an unwelcome passenger on the ride home.

CHAPTER THIRTY-FOUR

I n the warming flicker of firelight, Kurt refilled their glasses and shoved the empty bottle of Cabernet back into the ice bucket—sans ice.

He recapped his visit to town hall earlier in the day where he'd made his arguments for not foreclosing on the inn, assuring them they'd recoup the full amount of back taxes now that the inn was up and running again and would be for years to come. The assessor's office was to get back to them with an answer once they'd had a chance to consider the new information.

"I gave it my best shot. Don't know if I was successful, Liz. They gave me the impression I was too late with my appeal. Didn't seem like they were really listening—like they'd already made up their minds. I have to say, the amount of interest and penalties on top of the taxes is sizable. Even if we start paying what's current, plus a few bucks in good faith, it's going to take forever to pay it all back, and the interest and penalties will keep mounting. But we can't afford to do much more than that right now. So I don't know if they'll go for it. They might get greedy and not want to wait for what they're owed."

It had to work. Elizabeth counted on it. She was grateful to Kurt for taking on the role of advocate. It seemed he had a knack for it. And they were starting to work well together, like a team.

"I know you did everything you could. And you're so good at it. Let's not worry until we have to." It was in their best interests to stay positive.

What she had to bring up next could send them on a much different course, though. She had to ask, get it out into the open. It had been drawn out long enough and gnawing at her insides. She needed the truth.

Leaning closer, she spoke softly.

"Kurt, there's something I need to ask you about."

"Okay." The glint in his eye quickly dissolved into a look of cautious curiosity. "What's up?"

She sat up straighter, dreading the impending conversation. She couldn't put it off any longer.

"I'm sorry to have to bring this up, but I received a letter the other day that it is quite disturbing. I don't know what to make of it, so I need to show it to you and ask you outright what it means." With her insides feeling twisted from agonizing over the letter, she was surprised by her choice of words and how calmly they all fell out. In her head it had sounded more like, "What the hell is this all about? Why didn't you tell me you were engaged?"

She prayed there was a reasonable explanation. And that it wouldn't inflict harm on their relationship. Was she doing the right thing bringing it up at all? What if he walked out on her?

"Can I see it?" He remained calm, but she wondered if she'd ever really seen him angry.

"Yes." Her voice cracked, so she cleared her throat as she yanked the envelope from her back pocket and handed it across the table.

Kurt examined the writing on the front, then turned it over and pulled out the folded sheet of paper. The ring hit the table and rolled toward the edge, but he smacked it down before it could sail off. Snatching it up, he rolled it between two fingers. Did it look all too familiar to him? Had he never expected to see it again?

Without a word, he placed the envelope on the table with the ring on top and turned his attention to the letter. His expression gave nothing away. Was he starting to sweat?

Before long, he refolded the note and dropped it onto the table. His silence confirmed Elizabeth's worst fears. She felt her world slipping away from her. What she thought she had, never should have been. It was all a lie.

Sliding into the chair next to her, he folded his hands and rested his arms on his legs.

"Elizabeth, I can assure you I have no idea what this is about."

She desperately wanted to believe him, but could she? His calm demeanor seemed out of place. Was it his training kicking in?

"I can't imagine who would have sent this to you. There *is* no other woman. Frankly, there never has been anyone I wanted to be serious with—that is, until I met you. And I was terrified I wouldn't find—"

"Then who sent it?" She wasn't ready to accept his quick denial. Was it hollow?

"I'm telling you, I don't know." His tone remained even. "There's no one in my past that—I've never been engaged before, and I'm certainly not now. Besides, that's one cheap-looking ring. I'd never give anyone anything that looked like that."

They shared a laugh, which felt good to her.

"Liz, I'm being completely honest with you. I don't know who could have sent the letter, but what a nasty thing for someone to do."

"For sure." She scooped up the pieces and re-inserted them, warming to his defensive response, wanting to believe.

"Does the handwriting look familiar?" He seemed set on solving the puzzle.

"No, but that doesn't mean it came from someone we don't know. It would be easy enough to disguise your own handwriting."

"Yes, but there would still be characteristics specific to an individual that would be present even if the person was trying to write differently. I'd offer to ask a handwriting expert to take a look, but honestly I'd be so embarrassed to—"

"No, I would never ask you to do that. Maybe it's someone who's angry at me." She shoved the envelope back into her pocket.

Leaning toward her, he scooped her into his arms. "I can't imagine anyone being angry at you." He placed a kiss on the top of her head.

Elizabeth hated the turmoil within. Clearly someone sent the letter with the intention of destroying their relationship. But who?

And was the story completely fabricated? Or was she being naïve to believe Kurt's denial?

Their chat had provided no definitive answers—only more questions.

CHAPTER THIRTY-FIVE

Coaxing *the stubborn stone* from the bottom of the old fireplace surround, a tingle started in her abdomen and emanated outward to her extremities. Oh, the possibilities of what she would find. What could her grandmother have hidden with her friend? Something valuable to them at the time? A favorite toy? A piece of jewelry? Why had it remained a secret all these years? What could fit inside such a small space? Absorbed in the mystique of her venture, she didn't hear anyone approaching.

"What are you doing, dismantling the fireplace?" His voice was stern, as if scolding a child.

Releasing her grip on the stone, she sat back on her heels.

"For God's sake, we've got enough projects around here without—"

"Kurt . . . take it easy." Slipping the diary page from her back pocket, she held it out for him to see.

"What's this?" He snatched it from her fingers and gave it a cursory glance.

Rising to discuss the matter eye to eye, she calmly replied what she took to be obvious. "It's a diary page. From my grandmother's diary."

He looked to her to continue.

"It's really quite neat. It has directions on it to follow. Many years ago, when my grandmother was growing up, she and a childhood friend hid something and left clues in her diary. I never knew it existed until just the other day—"

"Are you serious? You're wasting time with a child's treasure hunt?"

She'd never seen him so agitated . . . but she'd also never seen him so worried about the health of someone close to him.

"Oh, Kurt. Where's your sense of adventure?" She tried to appeal to his fun-loving side, but he wasn't softening. Instead, the poke seemed to infuriate him further.

"Get a grip, Elizabeth. You're on the verge of losing this place and taking everyone down with you. We have so much on the line. I think your time could be better spent." He handed the page back, leaving her to resume her nonsense if she so chose. "I'm sure Amelia would be proud," he mumbled on his way out.

Yeah, but what's hidden may be of use to us. Even something of moderate value years ago, with time, could be much rarer and more valuable. It was worth pursuing. If it turned out to be something insignificant, at least the adventure of the pursuit was certainly entertaining. She'd just keep Kurt on a need-to-know basis.

Dropping back down to the hearth, she probed inside the hollow until her long, slender fingers swiped against a cold hard surface. With her rear end up in the air in a decidedly unladylike position and her nose to the hearth, she peered inside with the light from her cell. Sliding out a small rusted metal box that had once held shortbread, Elizabeth held it up to her ear and shook it. There was nothing more than a soft rattle as the contents caromed from side to side. Prying it open, she pulled out a folded piece of lined paper, similar to that in her grandmother's diary.

Eager to see what lay within, she dropped the metal container and unfolded the yellowed page. The handwriting was familiar.

You have followed instructions
And by all means should be commended.
But since your task is not yet complete,
The next step cannot be suspended.

No need to travel a great distance,
Just a mere few feet away from you,
The old Leopold stands as grand as always,
An old friend holding the next clue.

A compartment meant to hold
Letters, stamps, pen, and ink,
Perhaps a secret note from a lover,
Could prove to hold more than you think.

The old Leopold. Made of dark, solid mahogany that was painstakingly polished over the years, her grandmother's grand antique desk had occupied a substantial space in the corner of the drawing room, creating a focal point that nearly competed with the fireplace. Growing up at the inn with few other children to play with, Elizabeth never tired of poking around in it. It had been an endless source of entertainment. Small doors with tiny knobs, drawers behind the doors, and so many other compartments kept her interest until someone came along and shooed her away.

Apparently the desk still held yet untold secrets—but had been severely damaged in the hurricane and carted out with the rest of the furnishings in the drawing room. Gone for good. A local scrap dealer had done them a favor and hauled away all the salt-water-soaked pieces so they could start anew. It was heartbreaking to see the old desk being pulled out the front door, looking undignified strapped to a handcart. It took three guys to get it over the threshold and down the front steps. She was glad her grandmother wasn't around to see it in its final condition. The finish had lost its luster, and the wood was so warped, the drawers and doors would no longer open without a great deal of muscle.

So this was where the trail of clues dried up. A dead end. Had she been too quick to dispose of the old desk? She'd sought the advice of an antiques expert who told her it wasn't worth trying to salvage the piece. The damage to the wood was too severe. If only she'd known it still held a secret she needed to find.

Elizabeth wasn't willing to give up yet. She would track down who had hauled it away.

CHAPTER THIRTY-SIX

*A*fter retrieving the name and address of the junk dealer, Elizabeth satisfied Kurt's curiosity for what she was up to by saying she'd uncovered a few items in the kerosene shack of the lighthouse she thought they'd be interested in. It might not amount to much, but they could use the money. To her knowledge, he hadn't set foot in the shack recently and would have no reason to question her. He wouldn't understand her errand if she leveled with him. Probably call it a waste of time—a fool's errand—and her time could be better spent doing any number of items from the to-do list that seemed to grow exponentially.

The ride down to South Portland took less than half an hour. As she pulled up to the curb in front of a corrugated metal building, she double-checked the address. Right place, seedy neighborhood. It would be a quick stop, she tried to assure herself. And not something that could be accomplished over the phone.

The woman behind the counter, appearing as old as some of the dusty pieces scattered about the small showroom, looked up as the ding sounded on the door. She had the raspy voice of a pack-a-day smoker.

"Help ya?" Her leathery skin hung past her jowls. A dull orange-yellow No. 2 tucked behind an ear poked out from her thin white hair.

As Elizabeth laid out the details of how the desk had come into their possession and the nearly unrecognizable condition it would have arrived in, she noticed another, younger woman at a workspace in the back, all but hidden behind stacks of papers. She seemed curious about the predicament, pausing to listen.

When Elizabeth had finished, the older woman grabbed on to the edge of the counter and leaned in. Her bloodshot eyes held their gaze, and her mouth hung open slightly. Words didn't come at first. Elizabeth held out hope she recalled the piece and was merely tracking in her head where she'd seen it last before quickly ushering her to the back room to proudly point out the desk in question.

"Ma'am, you know how many trashed pieces of furniture we've gotten in here since the storm?" She didn't wait for an answer. "Too many to count. And too many to keep for any length of time. We don't have the space for them." Her pale hand gestured in no specific direction. "The vast majority of which were absolutely worthless. And a piece that size would have been disposed of right away. No point in keeping it around. It would take up too much room."

The woman clearly had no idea how personal the situation was and how her words stung. Another dead end. Kurt would at least be happy she'd have to abandon her search.

"I see. Well, it seems there was something left in it that we really need to get back. It's important to the family." Elizabeth doubted the elderly woman could remember what she'd had for breakfast, much less a piece of furniture that looked very much like all the others. But it was worth pressing further, perhaps to jog her memory.

"I'm sorry. But I can't help you. We're in the business of—"

"Wait a minute." The younger woman with a navy blue paisley bandana covering most of her head was on her feet and approaching the counter. "I think I remember the desk."

"You do?" Elizabeth was suddenly hopeful.

"You said it was a Leopold?"

"Yes."

"This one was in pretty sad shape, but I recognized it when they rolled it in." To the older woman, she said, "Mom, don't you remember? I asked them to put it to the side, so I could take a look at it."

"But they go through everything that comes off the trucks to check for stuff left behind," the mother protested. "They obviously didn't find anything."

"Ah, yes, but a desk like that has hidden storage that most people don't know about and could easily miss, even some of the seasoned guys around here. That's why I wanted to take a look at it."

Turning to Elizabeth, the daughter grew sullen. "I'm afraid I didn't find much—although it was fun exploring the desk. Must have been quite a showpiece in its day. Sorry for your loss. . . . Sorry we can't help you." After stroking her mother's arm in a loving gesture, the young woman retreated to her desk and the mountain of paperwork.

It had been a long shot, one she'd had to take. Elizabeth wouldn't have forgiven herself if she hadn't tried. But the reality of the abrupt end to the road was a blunt reminder her optimism often plagued her with unrealistic expectations. She would keep her failed errand to herself. No need to give Kurt any more reason to rein her in.

Returning to her car—grateful the local auto body shop had been able to crank it out in record time—she left the driver's side door ajar to allow the built-up heat to escape while she started the engine and fumbled with the buttons to lower the windows. Anxious to leave the sketchy neighborhood behind, she jammed it into reverse, catching movement in her rearview mirror.

The daughter appeared at the window with something metal in her hand.

"Like I said, I didn't find much, and I doubt it's what you're looking for, but this came out of the back of that Leopold, so it's rightfully yours. Hadn't seen one of those in a while, so I couldn't wait to explore it. Probably silly, but it brought back memories."

Impressed with the woman's integrity, Elizabeth took hold of the small tin, like the ones used for throat lozenges many years earlier. It had been flattened slightly, either in transit by the less-than-gentle hauling guys or the person who placed it in the desk, so it would fit into the tight space. It would take some effort to get it open.

Calling out her thanks as the woman walked away, Elizabeth took the car out of reverse and reached for the glove compartment. After some rummaging, she came out with a miniature tool set that screamed of femininity. The handles were white with pink roses on them. A thoughtful gift from Kurt. He didn't want her to be stranded somewhere in need of a pair of pliers or other such instruments. At the time, Elizabeth was amused by what seemed to be an obscure concern but stowed the set in the car to appease him. It struck her the rose pattern resembled that on the teapot she and her mystery guest had used during tea.

She wedged the flat-head screwdriver under the lid and wiggled it. The tin was not going to give up its contents without a fight. She repeated the wedging and wiggling around the entire underside, which only served to warp the edge of the lid, and it still held tight. Eyeing the pliers, she snatched them up and latched onto the lid. Jamming the screwdriver under the pliers, she yanked and the lid grudgingly snapped open. Tossing the tools onto the seat beside her, she cradled the tin in her palms.

Inside, a folded paper with water stains and the same familiar handwriting held a slightly longer poem:

You will need to take caution as you go
Step by step, keep your eyes on your feet.
Dangerous rogue waves can push you off balance.
Don't even try, there's no way to cheat.

When you arrive at the stalwart light
Move inside and let your eyes adjust.
Look for a board running perpendicular to the door.
Our word on this, you'll just have to trust.

It might look like all the others, but there's a catch.
If you press on the end pointing south,
The other side will pop up
And you'll be gasping and gaping your mouth.

If the compartment is empty
Don't spare too much time to fret.
Someone else simply beat you to it,
And you'll never know what you didn't get.

While not entirely cryptic, it sounded as though she would be taking a hike down to the lighthouse. She'd been there too many times to count and had probably stepped on the board mentioned in the poem many times over the years. What could possibly lie underneath? It dawned on her she hadn't been out to the lighthouse for a couple years. She hadn't considered what shape it might be in. Was the next clue—or better yet, the treasure—still hidden within its walls? Or would she reach the final dead end?

She pulled away from the curb and headed back to Pennington Point.

CHAPTER THIRTY-SEVEN

Leaving the car at the head of the trail, Elizabeth scampered down the dirt path, anxious to get out to the light, stepping over roots and steering clear of protruding rocks that could catch a toe and send her sprawling. For a fleeting moment she considered if she'd need the tools from her glove compartment but dismissed the notion of turning back in the interest of time.

The path had become overgrown, the victim of neglect with no one around to attend to it. Underbrush caught on her legs and overhead branches hung low, threatening to obliterate the sightline ahead.

As she reached the turn, her cell vibrated in her pocket, so she held up at the lookout.

"Hey, Kurt. What's up?" She leaned against the railing, idly watching small waves crest out on the breakwater.

"Hey, Lizzi. Didn't know if you were anywhere near the property, but I just got word that the state forensics lab is back out at the dig site. I think they may have their results. Either that or they want to do some more digging."

More digging? So the project could get dragged out even longer? Enough was enough. Time to put an end to the nonsense. "All right. I'm not too far away. I'll be right there."

Disappointed to have to put off her trek across the breakwater, she vowed to return the first chance she could and made her way back up the hill.

She could hear the rumbling of a large machine before she'd reached the shack where the pro shop was housed. She froze. They were back at it again. Construction delays were frustrating enough without getting derailed due to animal bones—or worse, a crime scene investigation. Which was it going to be? She almost hoped for the latter since it would probably be wrapped up more quickly. But then again, it would do nothing to promote a positive image of the inn. She was already laboring to polish the tarnish.

Kurt approached from behind and threw an arm around her shoulders. "Let's go find out what the fuss is all about. Shall we?"

His levity was almost annoying, but she appreciated his company. Buddy brushed alongside her, looking up expectantly. She ran the side of her finger up and down the bridge of the sweet pup's nose a few times. He closed his eyes, soaking up the attention. Once they were on the move, he fell in behind.

As they reached the edge of the work zone, the deputy approached with palms up and met them at the end of the walkway.

"False alarm. The state just left. Apparently the bones were an animal. A small deer."

"They came all the way out here to give us the go ahead?" Elizabeth asked.

"Oh, I think they thought it was only right to return the bones where they'd been found. The woods."

"Really."

"Yeah."

"They didn't have all the bones to examine, but they said it looked like it was a fawn. Either stillborn or didn't live long after it was born. Probably abandoned by the mother. Over time nature took over and, well . . ."

"Kind of sad, but I'm glad it wasn't human." Kurt's relief was palpable.

"Yeah, poor thing, but great news for the construction schedule." Elizabeth embraced the positive news like a castaway to a life preserver. "So the digging we're seeing is actually to get things moving forward again."

Sam nodded and offered his best wishes with the project before turning to take his leave.

Not one to miss an opportunity to get an update, Elizabeth stopped him and asked about the unfortunate widower. Sam's shoulders fell.

"Yeah—he, uh, his condition has been upgraded to fair, so his prognosis—at least physically—looks good. Of course, once he's cleared for discharge he'll be taken into custody and formally charged with his wife's death. The state of Maine doesn't take too kindly to assisted suicide."

She was struck by the irony of it all. "Such a tragic situation. There was never a chance of a favorable outcome. He was destined for a life of hell no matter which path he chose."

The guys shook their heads, but there were no words to offer. Sam stepped back and slipped out of sight down the path.

Kurt's arm found its place around her shoulders again, and this time it felt comforting. Leaving the lurching and snorting bulldozer behind, they set off toward the inn with Buddy trotting beside Kurt, who broke the silence first.

"So what are you up to now?"

One thing about being in a partnership, you had someone to answer to when they asked. But Kurt didn't ask very often. And this sounded fairly innocent, like a conversation starter, but she didn't want to divulge she was dying to get out to the lighthouse on what he would consider a frivolous hunt. He pounced on her hesitation.

"Ya know, dividing and conquering is often a very effective strategy—you and I heading in different directions and covering more ground. But in certain situations we could be doubly effective by tackling something together. What's the old expression—many hands make light work?" He pulled up and gently slid his hand to her upper arm. "We haven't been doing much of the latter—in fact, none that I can think of. I feel like we're losing touch with each other. And I don't *ever* want to lose you."

She hated to admit it, but in her fervor to keep things running smoothly in both of her businesses, she'd lost sight of the importance of finding time for their relationship. He pressed further.

"Why don't we work together on something this afternoon? What's on your radar? Is it something we can do as a team?"

Should she let him join her on the hunt? Would he pooh-pooh it and admonish her for being foolish?

"Lizzi?" His forehead creased as he waited for an answer.

"Okay. I think you're right. We've been so busy, we haven't seen much of each other lately. Let's tackle something."

"So what were you going to do next? Is it something we could do together?"

She hesitated again.

"Lizzi, what's going on? Let me in already." His features grew stern.

"Okay, I'll tell you, but promise you won't get angry with me."

"Angry?"

"Yes. I think that might be your first response."

"Okay. I promise. I will reserve judgment."

She took him at his word and blurted out the details of her quest to track down the clues left by her grandmother and mysterious friend.

"So you don't know who this woman is?"

"No, it didn't come up." She couldn't see what that had to do with anything. It figured he would latch on to missing information. Significant as it was, it wouldn't keep her from moving forward.

"And your next step is to head out to the lighthouse and take a look there."

"Yes, that was the plan," she held firm.

"All right, then. It's a beautiful day. Let's take a stroll—together."

"Really?" He seemed serious, but was he testing her commitment to the inn?

"Why not?"

"There's not something else that's much more pressing that we should be addressing?"

"Probably. But if we can't take a break once in a while and do something together—even something that's not on the list—and have a little adventure for the sake of adventure, then we've lost sight of what's important."

She took hold of the pinky and ring finger on his nearest hand, tickled at his unexpected reaction. "Come on, Bud."

He let out a woof and followed behind.

CHAPTER THIRTY-EIGHT

N*ot a cloud in the sky* to speak of. It was a spectacular shade of blue. A slight breeze off the water took some of the mid-summer heat out of the air.

Sliding her fingers into his palm, she squeezed, not wanting to let go even when the path narrowed and they had to walk single file. Kurt responded with a firmer grasp on her hand. Buddy had run ahead.

She imagined Kurt was assessing how overgrown the path had become and adding the task of clearing it to the to-do list. All Elizabeth could think of was getting out to the lighthouse to see what secrets it held—if any.

By the time they reached the bluff, she had let go of his hand to make better time. Only slowing for a glance out to the light, they pressed on to the lower half of the trail, pushing through low-hanging boughs and stepping over roots that had become more exposed from the weather. A rumble in the distance threatened to dampen their expedition. But a little rain wasn't going to deter her. She hastened her pace.

At the bottom, the imposing breakwater lay in front of them. Its oddly shaped boulders with jagged edges served as a rite of passage to the light, one that could easily render skinned knees if one was careless and didn't stay focused on her feet as she traversed. Elizabeth had the scars to prove it.

A few gray splintered boards with weeds growing up between them were all that was left of the kerosene shack once used to house the fuel for the light—kept separate so if one went, the other was at a safe distance. In more recent years, it had been used for general storage, but its contents were clearly swept away in the hurricane. Just inside the door to the shack had been the spot where the key to the lighthouse was kept; but, thankfully, it had been in Elizabeth's possession when the storm hit. Since then, she kept it on her car key chain as a frequent reminder of her childhood home.

Kurt's expression turned quizzical. "I thought you said you had found some things in storage here for the junk dealer."

Caught in a fib, Elizabeth shrugged and dispelled his comment with, "Oh, is that what I said? I meant the storage shed out behind Acadia." If she wasn't careful, the fibbing would get out of hand.

Eager to move on, Elizabeth fingered the key in her pocket to ensure it was there. It made a curious bulge on her leg. No sense navigating the breakwater if you couldn't get into the lighthouse. She didn't want to revisit what that felt like, even if the weather was calm.

Taking a moment to gauge his readiness, she tugged on Kurt's elbow. "All set?"

"Sure thing. I regularly run across a gauntlet of broken glass to keep my senses sharp. Taking a stroll along oversized rocks with lethally jagged edges will be nothin'."

"All right, let's do this."

He followed behind willingly. "If we get out there and back, totally unscathed . . . you owe me a nice bottle of red."

Elizabeth snorted. She was thankful he'd brought his sense of humor. "It all depends on if we find anything out there." She surveyed the gray clouds that had rolled in over Pennington Point, praying the rain would hold off. It was hard enough traversing the rocks without them being wet. They needed to get out there and back before it came ashore.

Her pup had wandered off, sniffing along the edge of the water. As they took their first tentative steps onto the breakwater, she commanded him to stay, counting on a plethora of new scents to keep him occupied. He lifted his head to acknowledge her voice, and then stuck his nose back into a patch of thistle.

At first, their progress was slow as they trod side by side, plodding along, stepping carefully, their feet landing on each rock like a child's game of hopscotch. She held back her desire to run headlong to allow him to get the hang of it. Was she coddling him too much?

Anxious to make better progress, she picked up the pace and took the lead. A third of the way out, she glanced back to check Kurt's location, impressed he was just a few yards behind. A quick learner, for sure. Agile and athletic, too. All attributes she admired about him.

She kept her focus on her feet—where they were landing and the lace that had come loose on one of her boat shoes. She'd fix it when she reached the light and was waiting for Kurt to catch up. A flash illuminated the clouds directly ahead of her. She counted the seconds before the rumble. Eight miles out. Hopefully it wasn't moving too fast.

Halfway there. She could feel the bulge in her pocket pressing against her leg. Back to her hopscotch on the rocks, she recalled a rhyme she used to say.

> *One, two, buckle my shoe.*
> *Three, four, shut the door.*
> *Five, six, pick up sticks.*
> *Seven, eight, lay them straight.*
> *Nine, ten, do it again.*
>
> *Ten, nine, a big fat swine.*
> *Eight, seven, pennies from heaven.*
> *Six, five, honey from a hive.*
> *Four, three, stung by a bee.*
> *Two, one, now you're done.*

Giggling at the sound of her voice, she was relieved she was nearing the end of the breakwater. Only a few strides to go and— her foot missed its mark and slid into the crevice between two boulders, throwing her off balance and sending her sprawling on hands and knees. A searing pain shot through her ankle. Pushing away images of waves overtaking the rocks and crashing on top of her, she wiggled her foot loose as Kurt reached her.

"You okay?" She was impressed he wasn't out of breath.

"Yeah, got it. Thanks." After quickly tying her shoe and rubbing away the ache in her ankle, she took his extended hand and let him pull her up. "Come on. We're almost there."

As their feet lit on the last few boulders, drops of light rain began to create a random pattern on their shirts. A flash backlit the clouds and was followed by a rumble that arrived sooner than the last.

Elizabeth grew concerned for her pup. At the other end of the breakwater, he had abandoned his thorough search of the grounds to take a stance with his front paws splayed on the rocks, no doubt startled by the thunder and concerned for his owners. Like a lot of dogs, he could do without nature's fireworks display and accompanying rumbles.

"Do you think he'll stay?" Kurt asked.

"He'd better." She held on to a sliver of hope that he would. Anything was possible, though. The young pup could be impulsive and unpredictable.

As she fumbled with the key, she assessed the encroaching waves licking at the base of the rocks. They were running out of time and had to be focused and productive in their search once inside.

Elizabeth flinched when the lock eased open with a dull thud, half expecting the key not to work. Shoving it back into her pocket, she pulled on the handle. Kurt reached from behind and took hold of the edge of the door and gave it a yank, allowing the heavy, musty air to escape. Inside, the light was dim with gray daylight spilling in through small rectangular windows lining the walls in a pattern that mimicked the stairs that spiraled to the top of the light.

"Spread out and look for a floorboard that's perpendicular to the door and—"

"Liz, they're all perpendicular."

"Okay, well, see if you can find one that might be loose."

They forked at the stairs and began testing individual boards with the toes of their shoes. A flash lit up the small space, and the rumble that followed echoed. The storm was nearly on top of them. Kurt became the voice of reason.

"We need to get out of here. It's come up quickly."

She thought of her pup at the other end of the breakwater. He was undoubtedly frantic with her so far away and the storm so close. Still, the possibility they could be at the end of the hunt made her stay the course.

"Okay, just a few more boards." She headed for the section right behind the stairs. Wouldn't it make sense to hide something where it didn't get a lot of traffic?

"Liz, now." Had his voice trembled? "This *treasure* might be completely useless—if it even exists. And you're putting us in danger because of it."

One of the boards directly behind the bottom step creaked when she put her weight on it. "Kurt, this might be it." Dropping to her knees, she began to wiggle the strip, digging her nails into the space between it and the board next to it. "I think I've got it." The more she worked at it, the more it moved. "Almost there."

Another flash and a loud clap of thunder.

CHAPTER THIRTY-EIGHT

"Liz, come on. Let's go." His voice was gruff.

Pressing on the far end of the slat, the closer end popped up enough for her to get a finger under. "Got it," she squealed and yanked it open and tossed it aside.

In spite of his obvious desire to abandon the search, Kurt leaned in for a closer look.

Grabbing her cell, she turned on the flashlight and peered into the small space but didn't see anything obvious. Was it tucked under the other boards? Jamming her hand in, she rotated it around but only ran up against a sand- and sediment-caked cement subfloor anchoring the base of the light and the two-by-fours of the floor joist. She pulled her hand back out, wiping it on her pants leg.

"Nothing." She sat back on her heels. "Someone else got here first."

"I'm sorry."

"I thought sure I would find whatever my grandmother had left."

"Someone else must have known about it."

"Or one of the handyman brothers, Renard or Gerard, discovered it years ago and took it for themselves."

"Could be. And maybe it was something useless to them, like little girls' hair ties, and they just chucked them without giving it much thought." He considered the idea then regained his sense of urgency with another flash and almost simultaneous crash of thunder. "Lizzi, we've got to get out of here. Now."

Deeply disappointed the treasure hunt had come to an abrupt end because someone had beaten her to it, she tried to refocus on their immediate situation.

"I think it's too late to head back across." She recalled riding out the hurricane with her grandmother, huddled on the stairs.

"Where do you think Buddy is?"

She snatched a breath. How had she forgotten about her pup? "Oh my God, we have to get to him." She dashed for the door. "Poor thing must be so scared." As she reached the handle, Kurt's strong hand suddenly latched on to it.

"No, it's too dangerous."

"I can't leave him there."

"Lizzi, he'll be okay."

"No, he won't." She felt her eyes welling. What had she done to her pup? "He'll be terrified."

"He's a smart dog. He'll figure it out."

"What if he doesn't? He's still a puppy. And I've left him all by himself in this. He hates storms."

Kurt's grip on the handle loosened enough for her to push on the door to make her escape. Over the roar of the storm, she heard a yelp. Buddy had been pressed up against it and jumped out of the way.

"Buddy!"

The waterlogged and shaking pup wagged his back end at the sound of her voice and slunk in through the opening. The two doting parents dropped to the floor and smothered him in hugs. Only his tail stuck out from the three-way embrace.

Elizabeth held on to him, his body shivering in her arms. "I can't believe he crossed the breakwater on his own . . . and through this storm."

"Guess he needed his mom." He ran a hand down her back. "How selfish I was, Kurt. What if I hadn't opened the door?"

"But you did."

CHAPTER THIRTY-NINE

As the storm raged outside the hundred-year-old walls, Elizabeth and Kurt waited it out, perched on the stairway a few steps from the bottom with Buddy wedged on the step in between. He was too nervous to lie down—not that he could have fit comfortably. With the incessant rumbling reverberating in the tall hollow structure, Elizabeth took solace in the fact it wasn't a hurricane. And the two creatures on earth that meant the most to her were by her side.

Scanning the floor for signs of water seeping in underneath the door, she felt a twinge in her gut when her eyes fell on the spot she'd found her grandmother two years earlier. Before long, they wandered to the individual floorboards splayed out in front of her. One, in particular, looked different. Was it raised ever so slightly on one end? Maybe the plank she'd pulled up behind the stairs was a decoy, a distraction. Conceding it was kind of an obvious spot to hide something, she wondered if it was too obvious. The boards by the door, however, were not. In fact, most people would walk right over them, without giving them a second thought on their way to something more important. Elizabeth grew tingly. She needed to take another look at—

"Lizzi, Buddy has something to show you."

She whirled around to look into the sweet face of her pup who seemed oblivious to Kurt's agenda. But there, on his royal blue collar, was a pink ribbon tied to it. Elizabeth looked more closely. Almost hidden in the generous loops of the bow was a gold ring with a sizable round diamond sparkling in spite of the dim light. She looked to Kurt.

"Elizabeth, I love you more than I ever thought I could love someone. You mean the world to me. . . . You *are* my world. I can't imagine spending a day without you. Will you marry me?"

Words wouldn't come. Grabbing on to the stair railing for support, she looked at the ring and back to Kurt. Not what she'd been expecting. "That's for me? It's beautiful."

"Of course, it's for you. A beautiful ring for a beautiful lady." He chuckled. "Wow, that sounded cliché."

"You had this all planned out? You were going to ask me here?"

"Well, not exactly, I've been carrying the ring around in my pocket for a while." He slipped the small black velvet box out of his shorts to show her. "I wasn't sure when the opportunity was going to present itself, but I wanted to be ready."

Reeling from the idea of a marriage proposal, she fell silent. Thunder rumbled in the distance. It sounded like the storm was receding.

Suddenly his dimple disappeared. "We're not on the same page, are we?"

She took his hand. "Of course we are. I would love to get married—to you—but how can we afford a wedding?"

"I think we can figure that all out. We always do." He stroked the back of her hand. "Don't worry."

It seemed they had switched roles. Suddenly, she was the practical one, and he was the optimist. It felt odd to her.

Buddy joined Kurt in gazing into her eyes, as if also looking for an answer.

She grinned. "You're right. We'll figure it out, won't we? Of course, I'll marry you. I can't imagine life without you either."

As they reached over the pup to hug, he squirmed and nearly lost his footing.

"Sorry, Bud." Kurt stroked his sides and whispered in his ear. "Thanks for your help." Untying the ribbon, he turned to her. "Let's see those incredibly feminine fingers of yours."

Giggling, she extended her hand, thrilled he was slipping a diamond on the other end. She wished she could scamper up to the inn and show her grandmother.

"There. It looks fabulous, just as I knew it would. You're a beautiful woman, Elizabeth—inside and out—and I'm so proud to call you my friend, partner, and lover."

Holding her newly adorned hand out in front of her, she couldn't resist asking, "So how long have you been carrying this around with you?"

He hesitated as if considering the most diplomatic answer. "I'd rather not say."

The two shared a laugh and then slipped back into each other's arms. Pressing her nose into his chest, Elizabeth breathed in a tantalizing woodsy scent. Buddy'd had enough of the tight space and slipped out from between them, padding down the steps to the door. He sniffed around at the same boards Elizabeth had been eyeing from the stairs.

"Let's see what it's doing outside. Maybe we could start back." Kurt seemed anxious to clear out.

"Okay, but first I want to take a look at one more board while we're here."

He shot her a look yet refrained from suggesting anything to the contrary.

"All right. Which one?"

"There's one over by the door that has caught my eye."

"Okay."

They scampered down the steps and knelt near the base of the old wooden door. Elizabeth used the tips of her fingernails to try to pry open the end that seemed to be higher than the other. She wiggled the board side to side. It wasn't giving like the other plank had. Then she recalled what the riddle had said:

It might look like all the others, but there's a catch
If you press on the end pointing south,
The other side will pop up
And you'll be gasping and gaping your mouth.

She pressed on the end closest to her. Suddenly the opposite side flipped open, and she yanked it out. Switching on her phone's flashlight, she peered inside.

"Look!" She shoved her hand down into the hole and slipped a finger into the ring on the side of a metal box. Tilted sideways to fit through the slot, it caught on the edge and fell back in. "That thing's heavy."

"Here, let me give it a try." Slipping his oversized arm into the slot, it scraped against the opening as his muscles bulged from the weight of the container. He let it drop with a dull thud on the floor. "There you go."

They stared at the small gray box with a simple lock securing the lid. Buddy turned his attention to the find and nosed around it.

Grabbing the ring, she heaved it into her lap, shaking it gently from side to side. The contents seemed dense, perhaps well packed, and not giving up any clues. "It's not obvious what's inside, is it?"

"No, not at all."

"I don't hear anything metallic. Nothing's clinking."

"You'll have to open it to find out."

She nodded. "Great. We don't have a key."

"Are you kidding? That lock is so easy to pick. I can do that in—"

"No, that wouldn't seem right." She grabbed his arm. "We can't just break into it. That wasn't the way it was supposed to go."

With a perceptive grin, Kurt pulled away. "Okay, Liz. Where do we go from here?"

"I don't know." She hated to commit to anything other than stalling. "Let's bring it back to the inn. I need some time to think about it. There's got to be something I'm missing. Another clue. Something I missed in the last poem."

She sensed he was disappointed he couldn't show off his lock-picking skills and was pleased he cared enough about the venture to feel that way.

CHAPTER FORTY

Thrilled to have the box in hand but frustrated to have been thwarted in her efforts to get to what was inside, she opened the office safe to tuck it away until she knew what her next step would be. As she heaved it off the floor, catching sight of her newly bedazzled finger, the contents of the box shifted, and the edge caught on the bottom shelf, knocking it from her grip. It tumbled onto the floor, making a thunderous clanking, landing upside down.

From another part of the inn came familiar footsteps in a rush to get there. Before long Kurt poked his head in the door and asked, "Everything okay?" His expression shifted from concern to amusement.

Elizabeth grinned, pleased with his urgent instinct to check on her well-being. "Yeah, the little box didn't like the idea of getting locked up in the safe so it tried to make a break—"

"Liz, look at that." He pointed at the overturned box.

On the underside was a strip of heavy-duty duct tape with the outline of a key. Elizabeth dropped to the floor and pulled up the corner of the tape. No key. Just the indentation where it once was trapped.

"Oh, geez. Didn't think to look there. Who hides a key on the thing that it opens?"

"Don't know. But obviously it didn't stay put."

"Ooh, maybe that was a diversion." She got excited at the new possibility. "It was *never* there. They wanted us to think it was."

"Or it's . . . still in the hole." They shared a laugh at the opposing way they approached solving a dilemma. His, more rational, logical, and thought-out. Hers, from the right side of her brain, fraught with emotion and zigzagging ideas.

"It's going to be getting dark soon. Probably not the best time to head back out to the light." She could be rational, too.

"Another time," he urged.

"I know, but what if someone gets to it before we can?"

"Liz, who would know it was there? It'll be fine 'til we can get back—if it was there in the first place."

"Just wish I had thought to turn the box over."

"At least it happened." He let her consider the possibilities for a moment before continuing. "Listen, I just got a call from the town assessor's office."

"You did?" She tried to read his face.

"Yeah, they considered everything I'd laid out for them and made a decision."

"And?"

"Apparently I was unsuccessful at convincing them to hold off on any further action to foreclose on the inn."

"What?" It couldn't be. Kurt was the master of diplomacy. He had a gentle way of dealing with people—to lead them. He couldn't convince the assessor to go easy on the Pennington family?

"I'm sorry, Liz. Maybe I went too far by asking them to forgive the interest and penalties they'd tacked on—"

"Kurt, you did everything you could. I'm sure of it. Maybe I should have been the one to approach them."

"Maybe."

"What are we going to do?" Losing the inn that had been in her family for generations was not an option.

Kurt remained silent.

"They can't just take over the property. My grandmother would—" It pained her to think of how disappointed her grandmother would have been. Ashamed. "I'm going to have to go down to town hall and find someone I can talk some sense into."

A voice came from behind.

Their loyal chef greeted them with a glass of wine in each hand. Red for Kurt, white for Elizabeth.

"Tony, what's this?" She accepted the glass.

"I understand congratulations are in order."

"Oh, news travels fast around here." Turning to Kurt, she half-heartedly glared.

He shrugged. "I was so shocked you'd said 'yes,' I couldn't wait to tell someone."

"And, don't worry, they're left over from dinner this evening," Tony assured them. "Didn't want it to go to waste."

"So this is your preferred wine?" Kurt seemed flustered he hadn't known.

Elizabeth grinned, and Tony couldn't resist ribbing him a bit as he headed back to the kitchen.

"Well, young man. Sounds like you don't know her as well as you think you do. Better get up to speed before the nuptials," he called over his shoulder.

Kurt looked to her for a response.

"Yes, it is. Pinot Grigio to be exact. I mean, I enjoy an occasional glass of red, but I really do prefer Pinot Grigio." She hoped she'd been able to diminish any of his lingering regrets.

"Duly noted."

The slam of the screen door brought them back to their duties as innkeepers. Trudging across the foyer, the deputy didn't remove his hat like he usually did. His scowl looked as ominous as it was focused.

"Sam . . ." Elizabeth braced for what was about to be dropped in her lap.

"Elizabeth. Kurt." He nodded to each in turn. "I thought I should let you know my men are on their way to take Guy Moretti into custody."

"Who?" The name escaped her for the moment. "One of our guests?"

"Yeah, he's Eli Hunter's manager."

"And you're arresting him? For what?" *Arresting one of her guests?* She snatched a section of hair and began to twist it around her fingers.

"For the murder of Vincenzo Sabbatini." He glanced at the sheet of paper in his hand as though he wanted to be sure he got the name right.

"You think he killed our chef?" Kurt jumped in.

"We have every reason to believe he did. Yes."

"Why?" Elizabeth tried to wrap her head around it and connect the dots between Vincenzo and Guy, the grumpy manager who'd scolded Eli Hunter for thinking about going out on a boat excursion. Was he capable of taking another man's life? And on a more practical note, if he did perform such a gruesome act, what was Eli going to do without a manager?

"Apparently, eliminating the chef was the purpose of coming to Maine. Moretti made all the arrangements and talked Mr. Hunter into making the trip as a well-needed getaway at the end of their tour. Moretti is well connected in Vegas, and Vincenzo left behind some debt when he came to Maine—sizeable debt—not something that would easily be forgiven. Moretti was asked—" He put the word in quotes. "—to take care of Vincenzo. The feds think it may have been to have his own debts wiped clean."

Elizabeth looked to Kurt. Clearly he didn't have the inside scoop. He remained silent and dismissed her with a shrug.

"So we've had a murderer in our midst." She stopped short of using the word "again."

"Yeah, well, I don't think any of the guests were in danger. He had his sights set on your chef all along."

"Still. Just the thought of it turns my stomach. I mean, Vincenzo and I never really hit it off, but I would never wish what happened to him on anyone. So how did he do it?"

"We found a handgun stashed in a drawer he was using for his dirty clothes. It had a silencer on it. We're running ballistics on the bullets, but I'd bet my bottom dollar that's what he used."

"Bullets? Plural?"

"Yeah, two in the back of his head and two more—"

"That's okay." She threw up a splayed hand. "I *really* don't need to know."

CHAPTER FORTY-ONE

Waking to darkness, Elizabeth struggled to breathe. Something was constricting her esophagus. A shape hovered over her in the shadows of the room. Her mind flashed to the woman in the gym. In the fleeting seconds before she grabbed on to the arms above her and thrashed at anything she could make contact with, she wondered if the woman had been murdered after all and if the person responsible now stood over her bed.

A flash of light and an ear-shattering bang split through the stillness from the other side of the bed. The death-grip hands loosened and slipped away, pulled by a body that landed with a dull thud. From the dog bed in the far corner of the room came a yelp. A sliver of moonlight outlined Kurt as he raced to the doorjamb to flip on the lights.

Coughing and sputtering, Elizabeth hauled herself upright and teetered on the edge of the mattress, squinting from the sudden glare, straining to make sense of what lay next to the bed. Blood pooled on the floor as it seeped from a hole in the side of the man's head. She didn't have to look to know who it was.

Her ears rang from the shot fired. Kurt straddled the intruder with his firearm aimed at the man's chest. "It's Sterling, isn't it?'

She nodded.

"Get Sam on the phone. Get him over here now." His eyes ran the length of the lifeless body, but he didn't waver from his position. "We'll need the EMTs so they can pronounce him." She took Kurt's certainty to mean if the thug stirred, he would put another bullet in him and save everyone the trouble of having to do anything other than an autopsy. "They'll get here faster than the ME."

As the gravity of the situation hit her—her fiancé had shot a man who seconds earlier had his meaty hands around her neck with every intention of killing her—she realized how close Sterling's head was to her own. And Kurt took him out without hesitation— seemingly confident in his ability to strike his intended target and only that target.

After she'd tracked down the deputy, they waited restlessly for him to arrive. Kurt backed off from his ready position and laid his firearm on the bedside table. Elizabeth remained fixated on the gun and wondered if it was still hot from being fired. Buddy had jumped on the bed and was snuggled up next to her, his warm fur against her leg.

"Where do you keep that?" They'd been sleeping together for a while, and she'd had no idea it was in the room, clearly within reach. "Don't get me wrong, I'm grateful you had it and you're such a good shot." Or had he taken a chance in the heat of the moment and gotten lucky?

Kurt smirked and nodded as if amused with her concern. "It's uh . . . it's nearby."

"What's that supposed to mean? Kurt, I have every right to know—"

"Relax. You're not going to run across it by accident. It goes where I go." He glanced down at his victim, looking satisfied there was no sign of life. "In my line of work—well, my former line of work, but still now—I need to make sure it's within reach."

Elizabeth decided to let it go. He'd saved her life. She trusted him to stash his gun where it was safe to do so. In spite of all the triteness of how it sounded, he was her hero. Grabbing on to his torso, she wrapped her arms around him, melting as she felt him envelope her in a safe cocoon. She didn't ever want to let go.

Before long, Sam shuffled down the hall and burst into what had been their intimate bedroom, transformed into a crime scene by the intrusion of a cold-blooded killer and his subsequent demise.

"What the hell just happened?" The deputy glanced at the bloody heap. Elizabeth let Kurt take the lead.

"Caught this guy trying to strangle the love of my life. Couldn't let that happen, so I stopped him in his tracks—dead in his tracks."

"I can see that." Sam stepped closer to the body and bent down to check for a pulse on the carotid. "Looks like you took care of it. No chance he'll be back for more." Appearing to realize there was another victim, he asked, "Lizzi, you all right?" His eyes went to her neck. He reached out but stopped short of touching. "God, I can still see red marks from his fingers. You okay?"

"I will be. Can't believe the son of a bitch came in here and invaded our home—our bedroom."

Elizabeth considered for a moment how her friend Lucretia would react to the news. Sterling had demonstrated he was an evil man, but in the finality of the situation there was no chance for redemption. She had to believe Lucretia would be relieved.

"Who is he?" Sam looked to Kurt.

"Jonathon Sterling."

"No kidding. Why did he go after Elizabeth?"

"I've got this." She took over. "Last summer I attended a wedding up in Boothbay Harbor—well, actually I got an invitation to a wedding that never took place."

Sam's brows narrowed.

"The inn I stayed at—the inn the wedding was supposed to be at—was the Inn at Boothbay Harbor. I met and became friends with the owner, Lucretia Livingston. The inn had been her family's estate, and she turned it into an inn. This—" she pointed at the body "—is her husband."

Sam regarded the sizeable man taking up the floor space between the bed and the wall. His mouth opened slightly like he had questions about the underlying circumstances yet didn't know where to begin.

Elizabeth continued. "It's true. Check with the Boothbay Harbor Police Department. I'm sure they've been on the lookout for him ever since he slipped from custody. I think they suspect he's responsible for the death of the groom-to-be because Sterling thought he caught him in a love tryst with Lucretia, but it was all a misunderstanding. And in his rage, he went after her best friend, Ana, from her childhood, and brutally murdered her, leaving her body in the trunk of my car. Probably thought he could implicate me."

The deputy remained quiet. Was the story sounding a tad too far-fetched? Had she left out any pertinent parts that would make it seem more plausible? She couldn't come up with any more details to corroborate her facts before Sam took over.

"We had every town up and down the coast looking for the car that put you in the ditch, Elizabeth. Actually just got word from Boothbay Harbor PD that they'd found an abandoned black Land Rover with the front bashed in. Registered to a Jonathon Sterling. Took them a while. Apparently he had switched the plates so they had to run the VIN." He let that sink in for a moment. "So why did he come after you?"

"Oh, I think he saw me as one more way to get back at Lucretia. Eliminate all her friends and then she's miserable—as if *she* was responsible for his misery, his shortcomings."

"And now his tirade it over." Sam shoved his hands in his pockets, looking like a spectator at the sidelines of a high school football game.

"Thank God," Kurt piped up, audibly relieved. "Now let's get the damn body out of here."

As if on command, two EMTs appeared in the doorway. Elizabeth reached out for Kurt and pulled herself closer. If it weren't for him, she would no longer be breathing.

CHAPTER FORTY-TWO

"*N*ot so fast. I've got to get crime scene people in here. It may be obvious to you what happened, but we've got to take the time to document everything." Sam turned to Elizabeth. "You wouldn't want your fiancé to go up on manslaughter charges, would you? And let me snap a pic of your neck before the marks go away."

Elizabeth appreciated Sam's thoroughness. The last thing they needed was for the situation to get turned around and Kurt implicated in some way. Although she couldn't imagine anyone claiming wrongful death. The world would be better off without Sterling.

The deputy allowed the EMTs to declare the corpse before sending them on their way. No one to save there. The medical examiner and scene investigator arrived not long afterward, a lack of sleep evident in their heavy eyes. As they began processing, Sam stepped into the hall and got on the phone with Boothbay

Harbor. Although their room was situated at the end of the hall, away from guest rooms that could be disturbed, Elizabeth was relieved he did more listening than talking.

Once the investigator cleared Elizabeth and Kurt, they headed downstairs to grab coffee and wait for the deputy to join them. Opting for something more soothing than caffeine, Elizabeth's hand trembled as she took a glass of sherry from Kurt. Unable to shake off a chill, she slipped into one of the new quarter-zips on display at the front desk, the inn's logo with the lighthouse embroidered on the left side.

Kurt got a fire going and joined Elizabeth on the couch. She leaned in, and he pulled her in close. They allowed the flickering flames to mesmerize them, broken only momentarily by the snap of wood and sparks flying out. No words were spoken. Elizabeth dozed in and out until they heard voices on the stairs.

Escorting the ME and investigator across the lobby, Sam held the door and whacked the side of the stretcher on its way by.

Joining them in the drawing room, Sam grabbed the closest wingback. "He was a cunning son of a bitch. I'll give him that."

Elizabeth sat up. "It's been a year. Where's he been all this time? And how's he been able to fly under the radar for so long?" She pictured him lurking in the shadows nearby. And apparently he was, if he'd known when she was leaving and plowed her into the ditch.

"Well, it's a lot easier for someone with means," Kurt said.

"Plus he used a simple, yet effective diversion tactic. Sent investigators in one direction while he headed in the opposite."

The deputy's pained expression told of his own lost hours chasing leads that dead ended.

"How's that?" Elizabeth wanted more.

"Had them looking clear across the country for him. Steered them off course."

"How'd he do that?"

"Not long after he escaped custody, he bought a ticket on Southwest out of Boston. Direct flight to Austin. Looked like he was on his way to Mexico. It's probably less than a four-hour drive to the border from there. It was certainly feasible."

"Mexico. Why would he want to go there?" She tried to picture a prim and proper Brit like Sterling south of the border in his custom suits and shiny cufflinks. He'd at least have to remove his jacket.

"Turns out, he didn't. Just wanted us to think he did. They figure he switched his boarding pass with someone in the gate area—probably someone older who was using a paper boarding pass—then walked out the front door of the airport. Southwest doesn't have assigned seating, so another passenger presented Sterling's boarding pass to be scanned as they got on the plane. The airline was probably paging that person to report to the gate for their flight, but he or she was already on the plane and never heard the page."

"And the person didn't notice he had someone else's boarding pass?" Elizabeth asked.

"Liz, they're not exactly printed in large type for the vision impaired." Kurt had a way of clearing out the minutiae in order to cut to the chase. He turned to the deputy. "So he's been back in Maine ever since."

"Most likely. But until recently, after they got reports of people seeing him around the area, Boothbay Harbor PD had been wasting their time trying to work with Texas and Mexican authorities to track him down."

"Clever. Even for a cold-blooded murderer." She could cut to the chase, too.

CHAPTER FORTY-THREE

Intent on shaking off her middle-of-the-night encounter with a ruthless killer, Elizabeth sought out a whimsical diversion and fetched the small gray box from the office safe. She plunked it down on the desk and gave the thin metal handle a playful tug. It wasn't divulging how to release its contents—not yet anyway. It wasn't going to be that easy. She flopped into the desk chair Rashelle would soon occupy once she arrived for her shift.

It was an ordinary-looking, rectangular gray box. Missing paint had been replaced by rust in a few places. A simple lock was all that stood between her and what was inside. She rocked the handle back and forth as she speculated what it contained. She imagined her grandmother and her friend scheming to hide the treasure, composing the riddles they hid along the trail, and scampering across the breakwater to stash the box.

Now that Kurt was involved in the hunt, she didn't dare head back to the lighthouse without inviting him along. She slid her cell out of her pocket.

"Oh my gawd, Lizzi." Her Brooklyn accent slipped out in her excitement. "What's that?"

"What's what?" She followed Rashelle's stare to her left hand.

"You're engaged." She'd made it sound like Elizabeth had exposed her to a deadly infectious disease, to which there was no known cure.

"Yes, I am," she replied, managing to keep her voice even.

"Why didn't you *tell* me? How exciting is *that*. When did this happen?"

Elizabeth wondered how hard Rashelle was working to appear genuinely happy for her.

"Last night."

"And you didn't tell me? Geez, Lizzi. Are you *serious?*"

"This is the first time I've seen you." She pushed back but admitted to herself she hadn't sought out Rashelle to share the news. Why should she? She didn't want to have it come off as bragging, so it was easier to keep quiet and let Rashelle make the discovery for herself—which she did.

"Ya know, if this was a couple years ago . . ." She took a step back and leaned against the doorframe, "I would have been the first person you would have run to."

Elizabeth emptied her lungs in a deliberate exhale and held off on refilling them for the moment. Her heart thumped in her ears. When she couldn't hold out any longer, she snatched some air and continued. "Rashelle, you're absolutely right. You would have been the first person. But things have changed."

"What things?"

"Things have changed. . . . *You've* changed."

"I haven't changed. How you treat me has changed."

"Well, maybe I'm finally getting to know the real you. I figured if I told you, you'd be so jealous of—"

"Jealous? I wouldn't be jealous. I'm happy for you, Lizzi. Couldn't be happier. I like Kurt very much. I think he's perfect for you. And you, of all people, deserve to be happy. . . . You've been through enough crappy things in your life. You deserve to have someone special like him."

Elizabeth thanked her, extending her wishes for Rashelle to find someone special so she could know the same happiness from finding someone to love, and they hugged. She only wished she could believe Rashelle's words were sincere.

Silence hung in the small space, and Rashelle looked as though she wanted to say something but was unsure if she should.

"What? . . . Something on your mind?" Elizabeth braced for what might be coming.

"Did you know there are twelve steps?"

"What twelve steps?" Liz wasn't following her.

"Twelve steps in that damn rehabilitation program you made me go to."

Her choice of words surprised Elizabeth. She wouldn't have thought anyone could "make" Rashelle do *anything*. "So you've been going?" The relief in her voice was palpable, even to her own ears.

"Yeah, I've been going." There was a grit to her words.

"Well, good for you. I'm happy to hear that."

"What you mean is, 'shocked as hell.'"

Elizabeth couldn't contain a grin. "Okay, yeah. You could say I'm surprised—but thrilled. I didn't really know if you would go through with it, but I'm glad you are."

"I am. But it's hell."

"No one said it was going to be easy. I'm proud of you."

Rashelle shot her a glare as if sensing condescendence. "But *twelve* steps. That's a hell of a lot."

"I'm sure it is. Take as long as you need to achieve them. It's not a race."

"Cute, Liz. Are you going to tell me it's all about the journey? Sounds like you're coaching a geriatric wheelchair competition where everyone gets a ribbon for participating."

"You know what I mean. It's going to take time, and the length of your *journey* won't be the same as everyone else's. Yours could be shorter or longer than the person sitting next to you. Harder or easier. So don't compare yourself."

"You want to know what the worst part is?"

Elizabeth remained silent, allowing her to continue.

"The religious shit they shove down your throat." She pushed past Elizabeth and flopped into the desk chair.

"Really?" Elizabeth couldn't pretend she was familiar with the program. She wasn't.

"Yeah, I had no idea there was such a religious slant, or I never would have agreed to it. I *hate* that part—not that I like the rest of it—but the religious shit has me ready to jump off the nearest—"

"Okay, I get it." There wasn't going to be any more jumping at Pennington Point—not on her watch.

"God this, God that. I'm supposed to confess my wrongdoings. Pray and meditate. It makes me feel like I'm back in second grade when my stepmother dragged me to church with her on Sunday mornings."

"Shelle, I haven't exactly been a devout churchgoer over the years either, but one thing my grandmother taught me was that we all pray to the same God. And even if you think you don't pray, we've all talked to him or her at one time or another. Nana told me you can call it a higher power, positive energy, or even just your gut instinct; but the idea is if you connect with this positive feeling or energy and let it guide you, you can't go wrong."

"Well, listen to you, Lizzi. I think you may have missed your calling." She leaned over and playfully swatted her elbow.

Elizabeth brushed her hand across the contact point. "Cut it out. I'm serious."

"I know. It just sounds odd to hear you talking like that."

Then it hit her in the gut. "Let me ask you something. The night that Mrs. Leibowitz called in a huff because Eli and his gang were making too much noise in the room next her hers . . . afterward I felt terrible sending you to take care of it. I should never have put you in that position."

"Because you think I would have been tempted to join in?"

"Well, yes. That wasn't fair to you. . . . Did you?"

Rashelle shook her head. "This may come as another shock to you, but I didn't. I did my job and left."

"I'm impressed." Could it be? Was she really changing?

"Didn't think I had it in me, did you?"

"I wasn't sure, but—I'll say it again—I'm proud of you." Elizabeth wished she had forced the issue sooner, been a better friend to her.

Their awkward moment was disrupted by the rattle of the desk phone. Rashelle slipped back into her professional role, picking up the receiver and answering in a silky voice, thanking the person for calling the front desk.

"I'm sorry, sir. You have a cat? And it's what? It's missing?" Rashelle listened. The voice on the other end was animated, bellowing through the earpiece.

Recognizing the craggy voice, Elizabeth could tell who was calling in a tizzy. She should have known the situation with the cat-toting guest wouldn't have a favorable ending. It was simply a matter of time.

"Shelle, I'll take it." She reached for the phone.

"Huh?"

"I know who that is. I was here when he checked in."

Handing the call over to her boss, Rashelle took a step back, feigning offense, yet appearing somewhat relieved.

"This is Elizabeth Pennington." She held the phone away from her ear at his initial outburst. "Your cat's missing?"

"Yes, I let him out to stretch his legs and get some fresh air like he does first thing in the morning, but he never returned. I'm so afraid something terrible has happened to him." He sniffled in her ear. "I've called him several times, but he hasn't come back. He *always* comes when I call."

Well, yes. When he's at home in an environment he's familiar with.

"I'm so sorry to hear that. We'll get right on it. I'll pull together a team to scour the property. We'll do our best to find him. Don't you worry."

There was no chance in hell his kitty was going to come trotting out of the woods. With all the wild animals in the area, any number of them would love to have a fluffy cat for breakfast. Her thoughts went to the recent coyote sightings in the area.

After gathering a few willing souls, Elizabeth instructed everyone to fan out, calling the feline's name. Boots. How original.

Figuring she was the most familiar with the grounds around the inn, she took the section of woods that stretched the farthest away from the buildings, not particularly hopeful of finding little Boots.

Who brings their cat on vacation with them to Maine? Or more precisely, who lets the cat roam around on a property edged by thick woods on one side and a huge cliff on the other? And now that the damn cat didn't return for his breakfast, Elizabeth and some of the staff were having to step away from their duties to search for it.

Elizabeth felt more annoyance at the situation than anything else, fully expecting to have to offer her condolences at the end of the search. She was definitely more of a dog person than cat. And although she didn't expect to find the fluffy feline, she went through the motions.

Armed with a sausage from the kitchen, she called out the cat's name and whistled. The cat probably didn't respond to whistling, but she couldn't think of anything else to do. Several yards into the woods, she was struck by the stillness. Not even the birds were active.

Trudging along, she was startled when she came upon a dirty ball of matted fluff with four legs. She called its name, and it turned in her direction. Elizabeth didn't know cats, but this one looked terrified—completely out of its element. Looking a few yards beyond it, she could see why.

The beast stood at least six or seven feet at its shoulders. His impressive rack had to be five feet across. Brown steely eyes sized up the diminutive human in front of him.

Never having confronted one in the woods before, she tried to remember what she'd been taught. Should she run? Could moose run fast? She had a feeling they could. Should she back off slowly? If she climbed a tree, he couldn't follow her. But, then again, he would gore her before she could make it very far up.

A slight breeze on her back meant he was downwind. The nostrils at the end of his bulbous nose flared, sniffing his target. When he snorted, she was close enough to see spittle fly up on his snout. Did he lick his lips?

With ears back, he pawed at the ground with dull thuds, making the unmistakable motions of preparing to charge. But where had the damn cat wandered off to?

Paralyzed with indecision, she could only watch as he swiftly closed the distance between them. At the moment she remembered something about getting behind the nearest good-sized tree, daylight was snuffed out.

CHAPTER FORTY-FOUR

A *muffled voice.* Strong hands shook her shoulders. Stabbing pain threatened to split her head in two. There didn't seem to be an inch of her body that didn't ache. The hard, bristly ground beneath her felt damp. Nothing came into focus. The voice grew louder.

"Lizzi, are you okay?" It was a female's voice. "Tawk to me, girl."

She could only make a guttural sound that sounded foreign to her ears.

"Liz, c'mon, girl. We gotta get you outta here." Another tug at her shoulders. Then Rashelle got on her cell to summon help.

While they waited in the silence among the trees, Rashelle rattled on about how worried she'd been when Elizabeth didn't return after they'd all fanned out to search for the cat. No one else seemed concerned. A few explanations were tossed out as to where their beloved innkeeper was, and it all sounded plausible to everyone—everyone, except Rashelle. So she had set out on her own, looking for her.

Before long, there was shouting in the distance, and Rashelle yelled back, directing the person behind the voice to their location. Soft thuds grew closer. Rashelle exchanged whispers with the new arrival who then kneeled at Elizabeth's side.

Kurt's voice was in her ear. She welcomed the warmth of his body next to her.

"Lizzi, are you okay? Are you hurt? What the hell happened?" He brushed his hand across her forehead and kissed it softly.

Endeavoring to put words together, she could only manage a ragged exhale.

"Take it easy. You're going to be okay. We need to get you— I'm gonna lift you up. Take a deep breath."

Without fully understanding the purpose, she took in as much air as her battered lungs would allow and felt his hands sliding under her body. As he scooped her up into his arms, she let out a mournful moan as her chest exploded in pain. On the hike out of the woods, she lapsed in and out of consciousness. Flashing red lights came into view outside the inn's front door. This time, they were waiting for her.

CHAPTER FORTY-FIVE

Turned out, *taking on* a full-grown moose during rutting season was not the brightest idea. Most don't live to tell the tale. Elizabeth, however, could thank her youth and her rugged family stock for surviving with a couple broken ribs and an impressive array of cuts and contusions. Her bruising included a pair of shiners that replaced the ones that had just healed from the car-going-down-the-embankment incident.

Having had her fill of the inside of an emergency room to last a lifetime, she was able to convince the attending physician, who thankfully was not on duty for her previous visit, to let her go on her own recognizance of sorts—a pledge of bed rest and abstinence from commanding the helm of a busy inn for a few days.

In spite of her aches and pains, Elizabeth couldn't keep herself from feeling guilty for lying on her back while others toiled. There was so much to be done around the inn, and they were short-staffed as it was. Concerns about the inn's financial health worried her; the mountain of debt she'd taken on in order to get the inn up and running was—in a word—substantial. With the inn as collateral, they needed steady income to make timely payments on the loans as well as the staff's wages, utilities, insurance, and property taxes. And she still needed to stop into town hall to make her case at the assessor's office. In spite of overwhelming odds, she was intent on moving forward, believing it would all work out. It had to.

Would word of the recent untimely deaths affect future reservations? She'd have to work hard to keep the inn's reputation favorable in the public's eye and a place where guests returned year after year—as her grandmother had done, seemingly with such ease. Elizabeth prayed she could follow in Amelia's footsteps and make her proud.

After much cajoling, she convinced Kurt to fetch her laptop. She could at least work on a new marketing campaign or review the staff manual and bring it up to date. Tony could send his ideas for dinner specials as well as proposed dates for special events like the annual staff Christmas party and the Mother/Daughter Holiday Tea with toy drop-off. She could also check on reservations and any cancellations and follow up with Rashelle. Were guests calling to ask about the goings-on? Was she handling their concerns appropriately? Perhaps Elizabeth should have Rashelle forward those calls to her cell.

With her computer on her lap, checklists and journals spread around her on the bedspread, and her pup by her side, Elizabeth began to get restless working remotely. Her mounting sense of helplessness grew.

Even though it was too early for a lunch delivery, Kurt appeared in the doorway with a wide grin, the small gray box tucked at his side. Raising his arm high up in the air, he held a key dangling on a ribbon pressed between two fingers. He swung it back and forth as if attempting to hypnotize her.

"You went and got the key without me?"

His face fell, clearly expecting a different reaction. "Well, you weren't exactly going to be able to skip across the breakwater and get it on your own anytime soon."

"I know, but you could have at least waited until I could go with you."

His shoulders drooped as he plopped the box on the bed and tossed the key next to it. She did her best to ignore the image she'd instantly conjured of what the rusty container would leave behind on the comforter.

"*You* knew where the key was. It wasn't like I figured out the next riddle on my own and kept you from joining in on solving the next clue."

Seeing him visibly deflated, suddenly her behavior struck her as quite childish. She was being unreasonable and needed to back off and find a way to make amends.

"I'm sorry. I just—"

"You just wanted to do it yourself."

Elizabeth knew he was right. She tended to prefer being in control.

"We're a team, Lizzi. You don't have to do everything yourself."

"I know . . . I know. I'm sorry I reacted that way. Thanks for going all the way out to the light to get it. Was it in the cavity where we found the box?" She tried to put a positive spin on her tone and leave her ego out of it, allowing herself to get excited about the contents.

"Yup. Right where you thought it would be. I figured I would lift your spirits by bringing it all to you so you could open it."

What a thoughtful, caring guy. How lucky was she to have him in her life? Silently scolding herself, she felt ashamed to have been so selfish. "And you have." Stifling a moan, she sat up and adjusted the pillows behind her. "Let's see what's been inside all these years—what my grandmother and her clever friend thought was worth leaving all those clues to find."

A smirk crept across his face as he extended his hand with a flourish. "Your honor, my dear."

Her fingertips tingled as she picked up the key and cradled it loosely in her palm. This was it. The moment of truth. She figured her grandmother was lingering nearby, eager to see her granddaughter's reaction. Elizabeth almost didn't want to open the box, putting an end to the anticipation of the treasure and the journey itself.

Almost. She couldn't stand waiting any longer.

"All right. Here we go." Slipping the key into the lock, she turned it with a dull click. Hesitating for a moment, she allowed her hand to hover above the handle, then gave it a tug. It didn't budge right away. She grabbed on to the side to get more leverage and tried again. This time the handle moved slightly, so she tugged harder. The lid popped open to reveal crumpled newspaper pages.

"No wonder we couldn't guess what was inside. They've got it wrapped up so tightly."

Kurt nodded.

Elizabeth began to pull away at the yellowed paper, slipping out a page at a time and tossing them onto the bed next to her. Small heavy objects shifted with each tug.

Taking a step closer, he leaned in. "Are those rocks?"

Puzzled, she nodded. "Looks like it." By the time she'd removed all the newspaper, the box contained an assortment of different-shaped rocks, all about the size of a small child's fist. "I don't get it. Are the rocks worth something?"

"Doubt it."

"So why have us go to all the trouble to find the box, just to have something worthless in it?"

"Don't know, Lizzi."

She was grateful he refrained from saying, "I told you so."

"Maybe it's a joke. I'll leave it to you to figure it out." Clearly losing interest in the hunt, he planted a kiss on the top of her head. "Gotta go. Got some phone calls to return. You rest up, okay?"

"Sure."

Partway out the door, he poked his head back in. "Oh, I don't know if you heard—or maybe you don't really care—but the cat ended up finding its way back to the inn."

"Great . . . to hear."

"The guy checked out and left without so much as a thank you for our efforts."

"Figures."

"Yeah. And I think he left with Mrs. Leibowitz."

"No kidding. That's an interesting match-up. Who knew."

Elizabeth watched him slip out, leaving her in the stillness of the room. Kurt didn't seem as unsettled about the disappointment in their find as she was. At times, she grew annoyed at how quickly he could disassociate himself from an event—unplug, in a way—and move on. This was one of those times.

It didn't make any sense. If the rocks were just that—useless rocks—then there was something else she was supposed to notice. Something else to figure out. One by one she removed the smooth, rounded rocks and placed them on one of the sheets of newspaper. Pulling the box closer, she examined the inside, tilting it from side to side, searching for something else that could have been left to find. Nothing. No note. No scribblings. Nothing.

Discouraged, she tossed the rocks back where they'd come from with dull clunks and wondered why her grandmother would leave them for her to find. Perhaps Kurt was right; it was a joke. Then why would the elderly woman go to the trouble of bringing the diary page to her? She was missing something.

Picking up the nearest sheet of newsprint, she noticed the date. December 8, 1941. Emblazoned across the front page was the Pearl Harbor headline. On the flip side, next to an ad for Woolworth's, was an article about the tree-lighting ceremony in Portland. Elizabeth inspected the entire sheet from top to bottom, front and back, repeating the exercise with each page in turn. There were no notes scribbled in any of the margins. Nothing out of the ordinary—except certain letters throughout the text were circled. Several dozen random letters had a ring drawn neatly around them in pencil. Giddy to have a new angle to pursue, she arranged the pages in numerical order across the bedspread with one on top of her pup, who didn't seem to mind. Grabbing a pad of paper from the nightstand, she began to jot down the letters in the order they appeared, hoping to make sense of them once she was finished.

After a time of trial and error, moving letters here and there for the words to make sense, she sat back to read the result.

You thought you'd found the treasure
And could now kick off your shoes.
We couldn't help but giggle
When we thought to plant a ruse.

You'll need to look much farther
And take along a hoe.
The next place you'll need to look
Is where stones are placed in a row.

Near where we enjoy lobster rolls
And clam chowder with a view,
Start digging under the fifth stone
To find what's old, not new.

The back porch. They'd had untold numbers of dinners out on the back porch over the years, feasting on lobster and clams and all the other delectable treats from the sea. It was one of her grandmother's favorite places to eat. She never tired of it. The stepping-stones leading from the back door of the porch out to the guest houses—at least the ones closest to the main building— remarkably had not been touched, in spite of extensive renovations on the property.

Throwing off the covers, she eased her body out of bed, wincing as she leaned over to scoot her shoes closer with a toe. Hoping to slip past Kurt and anyone else who would run interference, she slinked down the stairs and around the corner through the back porch with Buddy at her heels and counted to herself as she stepped on each stone. One-two-three-four-five. She planted both feet firmly. It didn't give at all under her feet.

"This is the one," she whispered, tingling returning to her fingers.

Shuffling to the shed next to her grandmother's garden, she yanked on the stubborn door and slipped inside, letting out a groan as her fragile chest flared in pain. Once her vision returned in the dim light, she grabbed a hoe in one hand and a sturdy shovel in the other—both well-worn from years of use.

Heading back out, she caught sight of a recent addition to the front lawn but didn't recall anything in the plans to add new signage. Had Kurt done something without her input? Miffed but intrigued, she made her way over. The closer she got, the more it looked like a temporary sign. Then it hit her. It was the town's answer to their appeal.

She rounded the front of it, and her body jolted when she read the words in black and white. THIS PROPERTY IS TO BE SOLD AT PUBLIC AUCTION ON THESE PREMISES. Her eyes glazed over, and she couldn't bring herself to read the rest of the details. Her thoughts went to tearing it down and throwing it over the cliff. Grabbing on to one of the posts, she blinked to steady herself and bring her vision back into focus. Then she noticed the last line. DO NOT REMOVE THIS NOTICE. VIOLATORS SUBJECT TO PUNISHMENT OF THE COURT.

It was really happening. They were going to sell off her family's property. Her childhood home. Her grandmother would be bitterly disappointed in her. She'd failed the family, the townspeople.

Glancing back at the date, she figured she had a few weeks to try to prevent it from happening. For the time being, she would continue her search and see where it took her. Buddy lifted his leg to relieve himself on the nearest signpost and then trotted along behind her.

Returning to the fifth stone, she got right to work. She tossed the shovel to the side and wedged the hoe under the piece of slate to loosen it, surprised at how easily it gave up after so many years in the same spot. Using the flat edge of the tool, she eased the stone up and to the side, away from where she needed to dig.

Buddy looked on from a few feet away, distracted at times by the occasional seagull swooping nearby.

Then it was time for the shovel. As she leaned over to grab the handle, her torso exploded, forcing her to snatch a quick breath and hold it. Her task was going to be harder than she'd envisioned. Once the pain subsided she shoved the blade into the packed dirt with one hand. It didn't penetrate very deeply. She fought to stay focused. Could she pull this off? She acknowledged she was working with a significant handicap. It would just take longer than usual.

"Figure you'll have this done by dark?"

Elizabeth spun around to Kurt plunking an orange cone on the third stone. He grinned as he walked around her to place a second one farther down the path.

"I take it you discovered another riddle, and this is where the clues led?" Always quick to catch up, Kurt slipped the shovel from her hand. "And this is where we're digging." He shot her a you-really-should-be-resting look yet refrained from scolding.

Pleased he wasn't angry, she nodded. "Yup."

As Kurt dug, Elizabeth relayed how clever Amelia and her friend were for hiding the last of the clues among the pages of the old newspaper. She thought of how easily she could have missed them altogether and tossed out the paper with the rocks. If the light had been any dimmer, she probably would have.

"Oh, and this is for you." He yanked on an envelope sticking out of his back pocket and handed it to her. Her name was scribbled on the front, but there were no other markings. Sliding a finger under the flap, she ripped it open to find two front-row tickets and backstage passes to Tim McGraw's upcoming concert in Portland. Even though Eli's tour was over, he thought she'd enjoy seeing him.

"That was sweet of him to do."

"Yes, it was." Kurt threw a shovelful on top of the pile and wiped his forehead with the back of his hand.

"So, he and the guys checked out?"

"Yeah, he had to head out while you were busy moose hunting."

Elizabeth was disappointed she hadn't been there to send him off, but hopefully he'd keep in touch and one day come back for another stay.

Before long, Kurt had a sizable pile of sandy dirt next to the hole. "You sure this was the spot?" He drove the blade into the ground and leaned against the handle. "I'm down about a foot, almost a foot and a half."

"Absolutely." Sliding the paper with her scribblings on it out of her pocket, she read the riddle to him. She loved how lyrical it sounded out loud.

He considered the rhyming words. "There was no other spot with a view where they would have taken a meal? Like a picnic table?"

Glancing to the table near the stairs down to the beach, she shook her head. "No, that's fairly new."

"And there never was another walkway with stepping-stones leading from the back porch?"

Elizabeth thought for a moment and shook again.

"Okay, I'll keep going. I just find it hard to believe they would have dug down farther than this." He jammed the shovel back in the hole.

"Wait a minute."

He froze, stooped over the shovel.

"You know what? That step-down from the porch hasn't always been there."

"What do you mean?"

"That wooden step—we used to have to step down from the porch directly onto the walkway. It was awkward. It was larger than a normal step. So years ago my grandmother had a wooden step built to make it easier to step down. It's still pretty awkward because now it's smaller than a regular step, but at least people aren't practically falling out of the porch. So there must be a stepping-stone underneath—or at least there used to be. So when my grandmother and her friend were counting, they would have started with that one."

"Okay. . . . Guess this dirt needs to go back in." His calm demeanor was admirable.

Elizabeth grew impatient watching him fill up the hole and reposition the slab with the precision of a diamond cutter before moving to the stone next to it. Itching to get into it and help dig, she could only stand idly by and watch the second pile grow.

After what seemed like an hour, the shovel hit against something solid.

"Ooh! What is it?" She could hardly contain her excitement.

"Don't know, Liz. I've got to keep going."

She leaned in and watched as he loosened the dirt around the object. It looked like it was encased in plastic. Finally he was able to wedge the shovel under it and pop it up. Down on one knee, he plucked it out and handed it to her.

It was much smaller than the box from the lighthouse. Struggling to rein in her disappointment, she brushed off as much dirt as she could before unwrapping the package. Underneath the outer covering was a metal box much like the last but measuring a scant eight to ten inches across.

"I swear to God, if this has junk in it . . ." Elizabeth wondered if she was wasting her time and his.

"Didn't feel like rocks. It's not that heavy." He stood and brushed off his knees.

"Maybe it's cotton balls this time." Her jab seemed to slide off him. "Hey, there's no lock."

"There's probably a key with a note directing you to the next box." She ignored his cynicism.

"Better not be." She shook it, but it made no discernible noise.

"Open it already." He began to refill the second hole.

Pressing the side of the box to her leg, she gave the familiar metal handle a tug. It proved to be rather stubborn, so she tried again with more force, and it popped open. Her heart sank when she caught sight of yellowed newspaper. Not again.

Dropping the shovel, Kurt stepped closer. "What is it?"

"Don't know. Whatever it is, is all wrapped up . . . and tight."

"Here. I'll hold. You unwrap."

"Thanks." She slid out one of the wads on top and peeled away the layers to reveal a gold coin. "What the—"

"Nice. That's more like it." Kurt beamed.

"Wow, I can't believe it. How many do you think are in here? The box isn't very big."

"Don't know. Guess you'll have to keep going to find out."

As Elizabeth opened them one by one and tossed the papers to the ground, Kurt held the box in one hand and the coins in the other. By the time she'd finished, he held a total of ten.

He set down the box and began to examine one more closely. "Nineteen thirty-three," he observed.

Elizabeth raked through the pile with her fingers and picked one up. The fronts were emblazoned with what looked like a woman in a flowing dress, and an eagle graced the back. "They're all the same. Pretty. Do you think they're worth much?"

"These look familiar for some reason. Let me send a pic to a buddy of mine at the Bureau—see what I can find out." Dropping all but two into the box and handing it to Elizabeth, he arranged the coins side by side on his palm, with a head and tail showing, and snapped a photo. "All right, let me get that hole filled in." He tossed the last two coins back in with a clink-clink.

Easing herself onto the porch step with a grimace, she kept him company. Her pup sat at her feet while she stroked his head. "Thanks for helping me with this, Kurt. I really appreciate it."

"You'd still be digging the first hole."

Allowing herself a chuckle in spite of the pain, she knew he was right. "Yeah, I'm glad you showed up. I know there are plenty of other things you could be doing."

"I figured it was the fastest way to get you back to resting."

"Ha! And look what we ended up with. How exciting. I wonder where they came from."

"Too bad there wasn't a note in the box."

She snatched up one of the newspaper pages. Scanning the columns, she hoped her grandmother had left them some sort of message about the treasure. Then she spotted it.

"Here it is. I found it," she announced, tickled. They've circled letters again."

"All right, why don't you head back upstairs and decipher what it says while you're kind of resting. It worked for you last time. I'll finish here and come up."

Somewhat reluctantly she followed his gentle orders—primarily since they were steeped in concern for her.

After spreading the newsprint across the bed, she carefully pored over each column, jotting down the letters in order. Once finished, she rewrote it in legible lines, flummoxed by the end result. It was the longest of all the poems.

So clever you are to find the treasure
You've reached the end of the trail.
Congrats are in order, a pat on the back
For hitting it right on the nail.

A word to the wise if you want to be wealthy,
Hold onto these coins and you'll see.
The longer you keep them close to you
The more valuable they will be.

If you're wondering how I came to have
Something so shiny and first-rate
Rest assured I won them
At the high school political debate.

As our country's entry into WWII
Now looks more than certain,
I need to find a safe hiding spot
Not just behind a simple curtain.

I fear Uncle Sam will come knocking,
Looking to fund his military affair
And take my pretty gold coins
Though I won them fair and square.

Tucked in the earth in this handy little box
Was the best place to keep them out of sight
With clues placed along a circuitous path
For my future family to bring to light.

Please use your newfound treasure
To keep our home in good repair.
It's the least I can do to say thank you
To my parents, Dorothy and Alistair.

CHAPTER FORTY-FIVE

Love, Amelia Pennington with the assistance
of Sarah Anne Wellesley
(Proof of ownership of the coins can be found
on the award certificate, which is in the back
of my diary.)

"Liz?"

Wrapped up in deciphering the final verses from her grand-mother, she hadn't heard the doorknob turn and was startled by Kurt poking his head in.

"Yeah." Jerking to attention stirred the pain in her torso.

"Just got off the phone with my buddy. He called me right back."

"Nice."

"Turns out these coins are pretty valuable."

"Really? That's awesome. Maybe we could sell them to help out around here."

"Oh, I don't think you'll have to sell all of them. Probably . . . just one."

"How much do you think they're worth?"

Kurt grinned. "Just one would allow you to pay off all the debt you've got hanging over your head—"

"Really?"

"—and pull together a nice wedding—"

"Really?"

"—and everything on your wish list for this place and still have money left over."

"What? How is that possible? What are they worth? What did your friend tell you?"

"He recognized them as soon as he saw the photo. Apparently, up until recently there was a huge controversy surrounding other coins of this type. These are 1933 Double Eagle gold coins produced by the Philadelphia Mint but supposedly never officially distributed. Another owner was taken to court by the Treasury, claiming they'd been stolen. Initially the government won; but when the case was appealed, the appellate court found in favor of the family in possession of the coins. They found evidence that a small number of the coins were released—probably to test the market—before Roosevelt took the country off the gold standard and the rest of the coins were melted down."

"So these are *really* rare."

"Absolutely, which makes them incredibly valuable."

"How valuable?" She couldn't stand him withholding from her any longer.

"Only one has been sold so far, and it went for ten million."

"No way." She wasn't sure she'd heard him correctly.

He nodded, and his grin returned. "Hard to believe, isn't it? Now that more are being discovered, the price will go down slightly but still be quite impressive."

Suddenly she couldn't form words. She handed him the paper with her grandmother's final note.

Once he read to the bottom, he asked, "Is this Sarah Wellesley the mysterious woman with the diary page?"

"Must be." She grabbed her cell and searched the name, scrolling through the results. "It *is* her. Here's her photo. . . . Sarah

Anne Belmont, nee Wellesley, poet laureate of the state of Maine for nearly a decade. . . . This is her obituary. She passed away a few months ago."

"But she paid you a visit a couple weeks ago."

"Guess she couldn't rest until the diary page was in my hands."

CHAPTER FORTY-SIX

This time, *Kurt recognized* the number displayed on his cell and snatched it up to answer. The background noise startled him at first.

"Hey, Mom. How's it going?"

"Kurt, he's gone." The rest of her words were garbled amid sobs.

"What? What's wrong? What's going on?"

"Oh, Kurt," she wailed. "Your father. He's gone." Her sobbing dragged on.

"No. It can't be." His soft words reached his ears only.

"I was holding his hand. I'd held it all night. Suddenly this morning it went loose in my hand. He was gone."

The man she'd spent her whole adult life with had been taken from her prematurely—after losing a child in a freak accident.

"What happened? It was so fast." His throat grew tight; he had to push the words out. Desperate to hug his mother, he grew painfully aware he was all she had left. Was she standing alone in a hospital corridor? A voice paging a doctor confirmed his fear.

"I know. It was much faster than the doctors had anticipated. I think he had resigned himself to his situation—that it was the end. They'd said colon cancer was unpredictable, so it was hard to give us a very accurate idea of how much time he really had. I think he made that determination on his own."

Colon cancer. Where had that come from? No one had said anything about cancer. Why hadn't they told him it was so serious? He felt cheated. Their insistence on keeping the situation to themselves prevented him from being involved . . . as he should have been. Had he known, he could have been there for him—for both of them. It yanked at his heart he didn't have the chance to say goodbye.

"I would have called you if I thought it would happen like this. He wasn't feeling well so we took the boat across, and his doctor ended up admitting him. I thought it was just for observation."

Damn it, the professionals couldn't tell the end was near? No one could give him a heads-up? He wasn't that far away. He could have been there in no time. Chiding himself for not checking in more often, suddenly the burden he carried from all his past indiscretions grew unwieldy. There was a raw familiarity to the emptiness that crept into his gut.

The service was simple—just the way David had wanted it. Held in the modest church on the island. A couple hymns. Kind words. Elizabeth was proud of Kurt for delivering a heartfelt eulogy for his father—one that never would have occurred if they hadn't reconciled.

A handful of locals from the tiny village came out to pay their respects. Elizabeth wondered if they actually knew David or were simply being supportive of Lillian, a fellow islander. Either way, it was a thoughtful gesture.

His wishes were to be cremated, so after the service they headed down the dirt road toward Lobster Cove, past the rusty remains of the *D. T. Sheridan* shipwreck. As Elizabeth stayed back with the rest of the mourners, Kurt slipped his arm around his mother's shoulders and headed closer to the water with her. She clutched the urn as though she wasn't going to let it go. Gentle gusts of wind tossed her hair about, but she didn't seem to notice.

They shared a private moment before slipping off their shoes and wading into the ocean. Kurt held the lid while his mother poured the ashes out. The hand with the urn fell to her side as her shoulders slumped. He hugged her and held on for a while. Finally they pulled apart, and she dunked the urn into the water, rinsing it out a few times. Replacing the lid, they headed back toward the rest of the group. Kurt thanked everyone for coming and asked them to keep his parents in their prayers.

Elizabeth hugged his mother and whispered how sorry she was. The three plodded back to the cottage in no particular hurry—much of the short distance spent in silence. Finally Lillian spoke.

"I miss him so much." Her words caught in her throat. "I don't know how I'm going to go on without him. I never pictured it this way. I think I had this unrealistic fantasy that we would live to be almost a hundred, and we'd both go at the same time."

"I know, Mom. I'm sorry you have to be without him. He wouldn't have wanted it this way. Why don't you think about moving back to the mainland—closer to us?"

"I don't know . . . I don't know what I'll do. I certainly don't want to be alone on the island this winter. The people here are so warm and welcoming. We've made some dear friends in the short time we've been here. I'll treasure our friendships always. But I don't know about the winter. It gets a little . . . lonely."

Elizabeth chimed in. "I'm sure it does. You could stay at the inn." Kurt's hand stiffened in hers.

Lillian's face lit up. "Oh, Elizabeth, you're so sweet. But I couldn't possibly—"

"Why not?" Though a bit blindsided, Kurt had caught up. "We could put you to work." He chuckled and patted his mother's arm.

"Don't be silly, Kurt. Don't scare her away." Elizabeth held her glare, then looked to Lillian. "Of course, we wouldn't put you to work, unless you consider giving us objective feedback—on the food and accommodations—work. And if you did want to run a learn-to-knit class for the guests, I'm sure they would love that."

"Oh, I don't know . . ."

"I'm sorry. We're completely overwhelming you." Elizabeth backpedaled. "And I should probably stay out of this discussion anyway, but I wanted you to know you're more than welcome to join us at the inn."

"Thank you. I appreciate it very much. It's a lot to think about right now. I'll give it some thought. Thank you."

Once they reached the cottage, Lillian invited them to come in, but there wasn't much time before the last boat was to leave, so they had to decline. They hugged until it became awkward and said their goodbyes.

Kurt's pained expression as they walked out through the garden gate mirrored the wrench in her gut. Leaving his mother behind, alone in the cottage where his parents had planned to live out retirement together, had to be one of the hardest things he'd ever done.

CHAPTER FORTY-SEVEN

melia would have been pleased her granddaughter's wedding ceremony was being held next to the garden she'd toiled in for so many years. Elizabeth had to enlist the help of the local garden club to whip it into shape for the special day and hoped it would resemble their rendition when she attempted to pull it together the following spring.

She wore the same gown her mother had worn for her wedding, thirty years earlier, which her grandmother had made. Since it was a Victorian style made from heavy slipper satin with a high neck and long sleeves, they chose a late September date so the temperature wouldn't be an issue. She fingered the tiny buttons running from the neckline down past her abdomen. Remarkably, alterations had been minimal. She'd chosen a veil with pearl beading around the headpiece with tulle that fell to the tips of her fingers. The chapel-length train could be bustled up in the back after the ceremony. She felt beautiful in the old dress. And through it, her mother and grandmother could be there vicariously.

Fidgeting like a five-year-old at a family photo shoot, Kurt stood at the makeshift altar fashioned from the arbor framing the garden gate, with Buddy sitting obediently at his feet. Two friends from the Bureau stood at his side. Her groom looked sharp in his gray tux jacket with black trousers, a selection of Elizabeth's urging. The gentle breeze off the water played with the white bows at the end of tulle strands woven through the arbor slats. A cool morning mist had burned off, allowing the afternoon sun to infuse the joyous occasion with unexpected warmth. A cellist, flutist, and violinist provided soft, soothing strains of Mozart that blended with the sounds of nature.

It wasn't lost on Elizabeth that it was two years to the weekend they'd held her grandmother's service on the very spot. She would have given anything for Amelia to give her away and share the special day with her. It was also the day the foreclosure auction was supposed to be held.

Her robust bouquet burst with a cascade of cool white roses, only partially opened in a nod to what the future would hold for the couple. Elizabeth wished she had been able to use flowers from the garden, but it wasn't meant to be. Amelia's rosebushes hadn't survived the hurricane and still needed to be replaced.

Although her walk down the aisle between extra chairs from the dining room was short-lived, with only a few rows on each side, it was a lonely one. She focused on Kurt's beaming face and plodded along, reaching out to take his hand when she got to the end of the second row, allowing him to pull her in.

Handing her flowers to Rashelle, their eyes met briefly, and she looked sincerely happy for Elizabeth. Perhaps she really had gone through a transformation and grown through her trials and tribulations. Behind her, Lucretia glowed, having found peace in finally being able to move on with her life.

Allowing Kurt to take both hands in his, she hoped he would ignore how sweaty they were. His were dry and warm. The strength of his firm grasp was comforting.

They each had written vows, which made Sam's job that much easier. Kurt shared his regret for not chasing down Elizabeth sooner and his fear of never finding her again. In spite of her insecurity from being alone for so long, his words ran through her, dispelling a nervous shiver. She was falling deeper in love with him.

Her vows started out with more of a traditional slant, promising to be true to him and make their relationship a priority over everything else. The lines that elicited an "aww" from the attendees were, "My grandmother, Amelia, and the rest of my family who could not be here today to witness our vows would have welcomed you with open arms. They would have loved you as I do."

Expectations were that the small civil ceremony would be brief; but when the deputy reached the part beseeching anyone who may have knowledge as to why this couple should not be united in holy matrimony to speak or forever hold his peace, he hesitated. The pause grew uncomfortable as he rolled the paper he'd been reading from and wrung it out like a rag. The small gathering of guests began to shift in their seats.

Kurt, who'd been locked in a trance with his bride, broke the connection and looked to the deputy. "Sam?"

Elizabeth watched as his head, looking decidedly naked without his peaked hat, shook almost unperceptively.

"Oh, no," she pleaded under her breath. "Please, no."

Her fiancé tried again. "Sam? Can we proceed?"

Their eyes met: Kurt's were imploring the deputy to move on, and Sam's took on the look of a desperado who had nothing to lose.

To Elizabeth's horror, he verbalized what was pent up inside.

"No . . . we can't proceed." His voice was firm.

Someone near the front cleared his throat as if he didn't sense a discord in the proceedings.

Sam continued. "No, Kurt. I'm sorry. But we *can't* proceed." Each syllable was deliberate and loud enough for everyone to hear.

"Sam, what are you doing?" Elizabeth kept her voice low, hoping he would do the same.

"I'm sorry, Elizabeth. I can't let you go through with this."

The guests had caught up and stirred behind them.

Did he know about the letter with the engagement ring inside? What had Rashelle done? Did she show it to him? They both had it all wrong. Or did he know something else that had been kept from her?

"Sam, please."

"No, Lizzi. There's something you need to know. I've remained silent for too long."

The only sound to be heard was the mournful cries of seagulls overhead. The moment hung with anxious apprehension.

"I should have said something long ago, but I guess I never thought you'd actually get married. If you did, I always thought it would be to me. I love you . . . always have."

Elizabeth let her shoulders slump. "You can't be serious. Your feelings for me originated when you were a child." The words hissed through her teeth. "You can't possibly mean what you're saying."

"Of course I do. I've known you longer than anyone else here." He reached out to touch her arm, but she pulled it out of reach.

"Well, that may be, but it doesn't mean—" She allowed her voice to trail off, painfully aware of the witnesses looking on behind them.

"I thought that letter from his former fiancée would do the trick, but apparently not."

"That was you? How cowardly. Did you really think—?"

Kurt took hold of her arm and found his voice. "Either way, that's not going to stop us from getting married." He took a step forward, towering over his less-than-worthy adversary. "You're pathetic."

"So, who's going to officiate?" His desperation had turned to defiance.

As glistening particles began to obstruct her vision, Elizabeth latched on to Kurt for stability.

A familiar voice resounded from a few rows back. "I'll do it."

Their recently reinstated head chef strode down the aisle and stood next to the couple. "It would be my honor."

Without missing a step, he took over for the humiliated deputy who slunk off to his patrol car parked along the drive. Turned out, Tony had become a justice of the peace at his previous job for just such occasions. This was his first opportunity to officiate. He added a personal touch to the ceremony, speaking of watching young Elizabeth grow from a curious toddler with an infectious laugh into a beautiful woman who deserved to find love and had found it with Kurt, a man of unflinching integrity and gentle heart. Tony charged Kurt with the boundless responsibility of caring for Elizabeth—both her physical and emotional well-being—to which Kurt nodded and said he accepted the responsibility wholeheartedly and without reservation.

To seal the deal, Tony uttered the powerful, unequivocal words, "I now pronounce you husband and wife." One of the dearly beloveds let out a squeal, and all joined together in exuberant applause.

The newlyweds kissed passionately, which flowed naturally into a warm hug. Elizabeth held on tight with her eyes pressed closed, praying she would always have the comfort of his arms to run to. When she finally opened them, she caught movement over Kurt's shoulder at the same window she'd seen her great-aunt Cecilia watching her leave after the hurricane. There was no ghostly figure, but the curtain panel on either side of the window fell back into place as if there had been two people watching over the ceremony. She imagined her grandmother joined Cecilia this time. Perhaps her parents were there, too.

As the musicians began to play the recessional, Elizabeth turned to Kurt's mother standing alone at the end of the first row on the groom's side with her hands clasped in front of her. Pulling her close, she whispered into her mother-in-law's ear. "I'm so happy to be part of your family now, and I'm thrilled to be able to call you 'Mom.'"

Lillian hugged her back. "I love you, Elizabeth. Welcome to the Mitchell family."

CHAPTER FORTY-SEVEN

"Love you, too . . . Mom."

Elizabeth's wedding gift to Kurt was filing documents with the state of Connecticut to dissolve her design business and putting her condo on the market. His to her was buying his parents' cottage on Monhegan so they could escape whenever they felt the need. Lillian was pleased the property would stay in the family, and she could visit her friends on the island when she wasn't busy teaching knitting workshops at the inn. The town of Pennington Point was placated with the payment of all back taxes owed, including interest and penalties, and halted foreclosure proceedings.

The summer following the wedding, Kurt and Elizabeth were blessed with the arrival of a healthy baby boy—who they named James David.

ABOUT THE AUTHOR

National *award-winning* author Penny Goetjen writes murder mysteries where the milieus play as prominent a role as the engaging characters. A self-proclaimed eccentric known for writing late into the night, transfixed by the allure of flickering candlelight, Ms. Goetjen embraces the writing process, unaware what will confront her at the next turn. She rides the journey with her characters, often as surprised as her readers to see how the story unfolds. Fascinated with the paranormal, she usually weaves a subtle, unexpected twist into her stories. When her husband is asked how he feels about his wife writing murder mysteries, he answers with a wink, "I sleep with one eye open."

BOOK CLUB QUESTIONS FOR
MURDER RETURNS TO THE PRECIPICE

1. What was your initial reaction to the book?

2. Have you read the previous two Precipice novels leading up to this one? If so, did the story wrap up as you had expected? What was surprising and what else would you have like to have seen happen?

3. What other mysteries have you read that were similar to this one?

4. If you could speak to Elizabeth, what would you say to her?

5. In a movie version, which actors would you like to see play the key roles? Elizabeth? Kurt? Deputy Austin? Rashelle? What about minor characters like Mrs. Leibowitz, the cat man, and Eli Hunter?

6. If you could insert yourself into the novel, which character would you like to be—one that's already in the story or someone new?

7. Does anything in the book remind you of your own life? An event? A particular challenge?

8. What character could you relate to the most? The least? What was it about either one that resonated with you?

9. Did any of the characters remind you of someone you know?

10. If Kurt's father hadn't had health challenges, do you think they would have reconciled?

11. How would the story have been different if Elizabeth's grandmother Amelia were still alive?

12. Given the obstacles Elizabeth faced, do you think her strength and determination would have been enough to enable her to carry on her grandmother's legacy as innkeeper if Kurt hadn't been by her side?

13. Could the story have taken place anywhere else besides the rocky coast of Maine?

14. If there was one question you'd like to ask the author, what is it?

15. What did you think of the ending?

16. Would you read other books by this author?